Leashed
Lightning

Leashed
Lightning

by JO SYKES

Holt, Rinehart and Winston
NEW YORK CHICAGO SAN FRANCISCO

js 983 Le

To Elsie Rogers

CONTENTS

Leashed
Lightning

1.

Triumph and Disaster

Tides of nervous tension roiled inside David Hollis as he threaded his way toward ring one at the far end of the exhibition building. By his left side trotted a miniature Lassie who never took the slack out of the leash despite the people and dogs jamming the narrow aisle.

"Hey, Montana, what'll you take for that collie pup?"

David looked around and spotted the speaker seated on one of the chairs backed up to the wall. The fellow was a member of the host club of this annual obedience trial in Idaho Falls, Idaho, and he knew perfectly well that Flash was a fully mature Shetland sheepdog, not a collie puppy.

"I'm waiting for him to grow up," David replied soberly. "I want to see how big he gets before I sell him."

The man smiled. "What are you entered in, son?"

"Open A."

"Good luck!"

"Thank you. I'll probably need it."

He would, too, David reflected gloomily. Flash had been a real hot-shot in Novice. He had passed the relatively simple Novice examination bang-bang-bang to earn his American Kennel Club Companion Dog certificate in three straight obedience trials. Since then, though, the little dog had flunked the Open test four times in a row, and if he flunked again today, his career in obedience was over.

David found a vacant chair between a fat woman with

a miniature poodle and a small boy. He hung his jacket on the back of the chair and sat down. He wished that his dad would come to an obedience trial sometime. All Marshall Hollis could think about was the money spent for entry fees and travel expenses. He couldn't understand that training a dog and competing in trials was as much a sport as golf or bowling or anything else.

Gently David grabbed and shook the long muzzle that kept thrusting into his hand. "You'd better pass today, you old Flash-in-the-pan. Dad says we're not wasting any more money, even if it is my money."

The boy seated in the next chair stared intently at Flash. "Is that a collie, mister?" he asked finally.

David blinked. He was fifteen, a sophomore in high school. He wasn't accustomed to being addressed as "mister."

The boy, who looked to be about seven years old, didn't wait for a reply. "He's an awful small collie."

David grinned. "I left him out in the rain last night. He got wet and shrank."

"No fooling?" exclaimed the boy, wide-eyed. "Aw, you're kidding!"

"He's a sheltie," David said, relenting. "Folks sometimes call them miniature collies, but Flash is a Shetland sheepdog. You know, like a Shetland pony. We call them shelties."

"Is he smart?"

"Sure."

"Are you going to win one of those trophies on the table?"

"I'm going to try."

"Can I pet him?"

"Sure. Flash, shake hands with this gentleman."

Although the sheltie had little enthusiasm for children, to please David he extended his paw. The boy was delighted. "What's your name, mister?" he demanded.

"David Hollis. What's yours?"

"Bert Norman. Do you suppose I could lead him around?"

"Why don't you wait until after I've been in the ring?" David suggested. "He's not used to you, and you might goof him up."

"Okay."

The youngster's cheerful acceptance of the decision surprised David. Most kids Bert's age were pretty obnoxious. "If you want to watch the dog that's going into the ring now, Bert," he said, "you'll see what Flash is supposed to do when it's my turn."

The dog was an Irish setter handled by a man who limped. As the woman judge directed the pair through the pattern of the Heel Free exercise, David explained to Bert what was taking place. He pointed out how well the setter stayed by his master's left leg no matter in which direction the man turned or how rapidly or slowly he walked. "See how quickly he sits when the man stops. He's well-trained."

As he talked, David's own tension began to slip away. The setter lost a few points for being slow to respond to the down command in the Drop on Recall exercise, but he did a beautiful Retrieve on Flat. Then, in the Retrieve over High Jump exercise, the man had to give two commands before the setter would jump over the barrier to retrieve his dumbbell. David groaned. "That flunks him!"

"Why? He got it, and he brought it back."

"Yes, but he didn't do it on the first command. You're only allowed to tell your dog once."

"Gee, can Flash do that? That's an awful high jump for a little dog."

David smiled. "Flash only has to jump half again his own shoulder height. Big dogs go over big jumps and little dogs go over little jumps."

The setter performed the last of the individual exercises, the Broad Jump, and the spectators applauded as he came out of the ring. David stood up.

"Are you next?" Bert wanted to know.

"No, there's one more before me. I just want to move around a little."

He scanned the room for a sight of his best friend. Johnny Martz had taken his big tri-color collie outside for exercise but had promised to be back in time to watch Flash. A crowd had gathered just inside the main entrance to the building, and presently David spotted Johnny's dad. Mr. Martz was a real swell guy. Unlike David's father, he was never too busy to do things with his family. Just now, as he hurried toward David, he seemed out of breath.

"Oh, there you are, David. Johnny asked me to tell you he's coming. There's a big mongrel loose on the grounds—looks like a part-Chesapeake. It and Shad got into a little disagreement. Johnny's with the vet now getting his dog patched up."

"How bad is Shad hurt?" David demanded in swift alarm. His friend's collie was a show prospect as well as an obedience dog. A single snap of hostile jaws could ruin a perfect ear and end a promising show career.

"He has a torn lip. It didn't look too serious."

"What'd they do about the other dog?"

"They had to settle for running him off. The ground-keepers tried to catch him, but they couldn't get near him."

Someone touched David on the arm. He turned as one of the stewards from ring one said, "Number forty-seven, you're up next. Just a couple of minutes."

David thanked the man and twisted to see that he had his arm band on right side up. "Oh, I've got to get my dumbbell," he exclaimed, remembering suddenly. "There's another chair over here, Mr. Martz."

He got the hardwood dumbbell from his jacket pocket and heeled Flash over to the entrance of the obedience ring. Feeling all quivery inside, he bent to slap the little dog in rough affection. "Are you going to work for me today, ol' buddy?"

Flash snapped at the air and wriggled his whole body in delight. Actually, there was only one exercise that really worried David. He had worked his dog nearly every day all summer long in preparation for this trial, and Flash was sharp. Three weeks ago, however, David had put on a demonstration for a men's club, and the sheltie had slipped on a polished floor while attempting the broad jump. He had taken a bad fall, and as a result he had been half-frightened of broad jumping ever since.

Just as the woman ahead of David finished, Johnny Martz put in an appearance. His thatch of astonishing red hair topped his tall, skinny frame like a beacon. Swiftly he made his way to ringside, a huge tri-color collie nervously pressing against him.

"Boy, I barely made it," he greeted David. "Good luck, now!"

David had no time to reply as a steward motioned him into the ring. While the judge was busy subtotaling the score of the previous contestant, David took his place for the start of the heeling exercise. He handed his leash and Flash's dumbbell to the steward. Then he waited, hoping his inner tension would not upset his dog.

By the time the jumps had been adjusted for Flash, the judge was ready. She was a large woman with gray hair and a pleasant smile. She checked her book against David's arm band before speaking. "Another sheltie. Did you see that beautiful-working sheltie in my Utility class?"

David nodded. The dog had not been nearly as handsome as Flash, but it had been well-trained. "I hope mine will do half as well," he said.

Obedience judges, he had discovered, nearly always tried to put you at ease. Although David appreciated their good intentions, he could never loosen up until he was actually into the test, and then he was too busy trying to do the right thing to worry about doing the wrong thing. He glanced at Flash. The sheltie was sitting squarely on his haunches, eyes and ears alert.

"The first exercise is the Heel Free. Are you ready?"

Again David bobbed his head in the affirmative.

"All right. Forward!"

"Flash, heel!"

He felt rather than saw that his dog moved with him. A handler wasn't supposed to watch his dog; he was supposed to have confidence.

"Halt!" the judge ordered.

Now David stole a glance out of the corner of his eye. Flash was right beside him, sitting straight, his collie-like head tilted upward in an attitude of eager expectancy.

Again the judge started them forward. Striding with them, she called for a left turn as they came to the end of the ring, another left turn at the corner, then, "Fast pace!"

Like a machine David eased into a run.

"Normal . . . About turn . . . Right turn . . . Halt."

David tried not to anticipate commands. He knew his every response affected the smoothness of his dog's performance. He scarcely drew a whole breath until the final halt and "Exercise finished."

"Figure Eight!" said the judge.

As two stewards hurried into the ring to station them selves about eight feet apart, David took advantage of t momentary break to praise Flash. The figure eight exe cise was designed to show how a dog would adapt pace to avoid either tripping his master or lagging behi David and Flash had practiced walking circles aro trees, friends, even bridge lamps.

The judge smiled. "Ready?"

This part of the heeling exercise took only a mi With its conclusion David roughed Flash affection and exclaimed in approval. So far, so good!

"The Drop on Recall is next," said the judge. "I'l you take your dog up there." She pointed. "When you to call him, I'll give you a hand signal, like so him as nearly opposite me as you can."

David nodded his understanding. Ordering F heel, he walked to the far end of the ring. Last sp

the Montana Copper Circuit, this was the exercise that had stopped the sheltie twice. He'd been real good of late, though, if he just wouldn't anticipate the down!

"You watch me and wait for my signal, old buddy," he warned softly.

Flash wagged his tail and clicked his jaws in that love snap he reserved for David alone.

The judge had taken a position to one side and a little better than halfway down the length of the ring. "Ready?" she called.

"Yes," David answered.

"Leave your dog!"

With his left hand David made a blocking motion in front of the sheltie's nose. "Stay!" he ordered with special emphasis. He thought as he stepped away of the many times he had seen other people's dogs stand up or lie down behind their masters, or even follow their handlers. Then he turned at the far end of the ring and drew a breath of relief to see that Flash was still sitting as he had left him.

Using an unobtrusive hand movement, the judge indicated for him to call his dog.

"Flash, come!"

A sable streak, the little dog bounded forward. David watched, gauging. When the sheltie was almost even with the judge, he raised his right hand in an abrupt, threatening manner, and breathed again when Flash dropped as if he had been shot.

The judge waited a few seconds to see if the dog would creep forward or, worse yet, stand up and continue on to his master without a command, but Flash laid his muzzle

on the floor and moved his plumed tail ever so slightly.

Again the judge motioned for David to call his dog.

"Flash, come!"

Jaws gaily parted, the sheltie came in. As he sat in front of David, his white forefeet almost touching David's toes, he snapped again in delight.

"Finish," said the judge, smiling.

Without speaking, David made a sharp hand motion to his left side. Flash jumped, pivoting in mid-air, and sat smartly at the heel position.

"Exercise finished."

Joyfully, David bent to love up his dog. Flash was outdoing himself. "You old faker. You old Flashy faker!"

The ring steward brought the dumbbell for the retrieving exercises, and David ordered the sheltie to heel again. "Are you ready?" asked the judge.

Without a wrong move, Flash performed the Retrieve on Flat and the Retrieve over High Jump. He loved to "get it" and to carry, and he liked jumping the high barrier. His very enthusiasm made him exciting to watch. David allowed himself a warm glow of pride.

Then they faced the Broad Jump. If they could pass this exercise, David knew the rest of the way was clear sailing. Only the group exercises remained, and Flash had never broken a Long Sit or Long Down in his life.

For Flash the broad jump was composed of three hurdles. Each was about five feet long and they were laid side by side, the space between determining the over-all length of the jump. David thought when he approached it that the span looked awfully long for his small dog, but he knew that the stewards had measured carefully. The distance was exactly double the height of the high jump. Each dog was required to jump according to his own size.

"Ready?" asked the judge.

"I hope so," David responded.

"Leave your dog."

Telling Flash to stay, David left him sitting about eight feet from the jump. With inward trembling, he moved to the right side of the flat rectangle formed by the three hurdles and took his position beside it and facing it. A strip of black rubber matting offered good footing for the dogs. If fear of slipping did not prevent his trying, Flash should clear the jump without difficulty.

"Send your dog!"

David drew in a long breath and released part of it. He put all the authority possible into his command without letting his voice sound harsh. "Flash, jump!"

Flash grinned as only a sheltie or a collie can grin. He sprang forward and launched himself as if he meant to clear the Panama Canal. David turned as his dog sailed by. Flash landed cleanly and swung back promptly to come and sit in front of his master. He topped the perfection of his performance with an impish snap of his gleaming eyeteeth.

"Finish," commanded the judge.

"Flash, heel!"

David was so elated that he failed for a second to comprehend why the judge suddenly frowned. He looked down at his side and was shocked to see Flash sitting almost behind him, the alert sheltie head peering around his leg, waiting for the praise and release that were sure to come.

"Exercise finished," said the judge. "Oh, you bad **boy,**

Flash," she scolded. "You did everything else so beautifully!"

In delight David pounded his dog. Who cared about one sloppy sit? It couldn't cost him more than a point. Clearing the broad jump was the important thing, and Flash hadn't hesitated. Applause rolled in his ears as he accepted his leash and dumbbell from the steward and strode from the ring.

Johnny and Mr. Martz met him at the gate. "That's the high score so far!" Johnny exclaimed. "Man, he was just perfect!"

"You really looked good out there," Mr. Martz affirmed.

David grinned broadly. "I do think he's improved since last spring."

"I'll betcha he goes High Score in Trial!" Johnny declared.

"Boy, wouldn't that be something! Dad sure couldn't kick about that, could he!"

David walked over to the chair where he had left his jacket and was greeted by a beaming little boy. "Flash is the smartest dog of all, isn't he, David? Everybody says he did the best. I saved your chair for you, David."

"Who's this, your cheering section?" Johnny asked over his shoulder.

David introduced the two—his best friend and his small admirer. "After the stays, Bert and I are going to take Flash out and walk him around," he explained.

"Make him pay you, Bert," Johnny advised in mock seriousness. "It's beginning to rain."

The last dog to work in Open A was a majestic standard poodle. As they watched him perform, Johnny predicted, "He'll get his leg, easy."

"What'll get his leg?" Bert asked.

"The poodle. Oh . . ." Johnny laughed suddenly. "You tell him, David. I'm never any good at explaining things."

David remembered his own ignorance a couple of years ago. "When a dog passes one of these tests," he said patiently, "he earns what they call a leg. When he gets three legs under three different judges, he gets a sort of diploma, and then he can work on the next test. Johnny's dog has two legs in Novice. If he passes today, he'll get his Companion Dog certificate."

"How many legs does Flash have?"

"None in Open. He already has his Companion Dog degree, and he's trying to get to be a Companion Dog Excellent."

As the poodle finished, the onlookers applauded, and David got in line to go back into the ring for the Long Sit and Long Down. He felt certain he had no reason to worry, and yet if he had learned anything about dogs, he had learned you must always expect the unexpected.

While the judge prepared her scoring sheets, the stewards lined up the seven Open A dogs and their handlers. Leashes and arm bands were placed behind the dogs. "The Long Sit," said the judge when she was ready, "is for three minutes. When I tell you to leave your dogs, you will cross the ring to the opposite side, make a right turn, and follow the steward in single file. He will lead you outside the building, where you will stay out of sight of your dogs until I signal for your return."

The judge paused. "When you come back into the ring you will line up across from your dogs and wait until I give the command for you to return to your dogs. Are there any questions?"

No one spoke up and the judge smiled. "Ready? Sit your dogs!"

Most of the dogs were already sitting at heel, but the handlers bent over them for last-minute positioning.

"Leave your dogs!"

A chorus of "stays" sounded as seven voices gave the same command. David strode across the ring in line with the other handlers. As he turned to file out the gate, he glanced back at the row of dogs. Each one was sitting straight and alert, his eyes on his master. Flash looked awfully small between a German shepherd on his right and the standard poodle on his left.

Spectators stood aside as the ring steward led them to the door. "The Irish setter is down," David heard someone say.

The man who owned the Irish setter groaned and looked back. "You big prune!" he murmured in disgust.

The September sun had vanished behind lowering gray masses. The air was chill with a touch of moisture in it, and the wet grass gave evidence of a shower just past. "What time is it?" somebody asked.

"Twelve-thirty, exactly."

The seven of them stood together and talked of their own and each other's dogs. "Thought I had a leg for sure today," said the owner of the Irish setter. "Anybody want to buy a big red dog cheap?"

"I'll trade you a miniature poodle that has now blown nine trials in a row," said a pleasant-faced woman in loud striped slacks.

"Do they offer a trophy for the lowest scoring dog in trial?"

"Flunk early and relax, I always say. Schatzi saw a

candy wrapper outside the ring and left me on the Heel Free."

At the door the ring steward checked his watch. "About time," he warned, and a second later snapped, "Come on!"

In reverse order they filed back into the building. David breathed a sigh of relief at the sight of Flash sitting exactly as he had left him. Only the setter had broken the sit-stay.

The Long Down was for five minutes. David spent the five-minute wait outside the door trying to guess the placing of the top three dogs. Four trophies would be given, but four of the seven dogs had flunked one or more exercises; so the fourth-place trophy would be won by a non-qualifying score. Only Flash, the German shepherd, and the standard poodle had qualified in all exercises—assuming none of the three blew the Long Down.

The owner of the poodle might have been reading David's thoughts. "Your sheltie certainly looked sharp. I believe he's in first place."

"That's because my Dad threatened him," David replied with a smile. "He's had lots of practice flunking."

When they trooped back inside, all the dogs were still down. Johnny caught David's eye and clasped his hands over his head in an enthusiastic victory signal.

"Please stay in the ring, everybody," said the steward. "We'll have the placings in just a minute."

The judge seemed to take forever tallying the scores, but finally she stood up to address spectators as well as contestants. "I have completed the judging of Open A class. A perfect score in this class is two hundred points. To qualify for a leg toward the Companion Dog Excellent certificate, a dog must score over fifty per cent of the available points in each of the seven exercises and earn a total score of not less than one hundred and seventy points. Three of the dogs in this class have earned qualifying scores."

As he listened, David caught the muscles of his fingers tightening into knots. Consciously he made himself relax. The tension would be over in a few seconds. Back home, in local obedience classes, the master of ceremonies would always announce the fourth place winner first and then work up to the number-one dog and handler, but A.K.C. judges were not concerned with building suspense.

"The first-place dog in Open A . . . with a score of 199½ is . . ."

David twisted his neck to look at his arm band.

". . . Dog number forty-seven."

With a whoop of joy David stepped forward to receive his awards. The judge smiled as she handed him the blue ribbon and the gleaming fourteen-inch trophy. "If it hadn't been for that one sit, I'd have given him a perfect score. You have a beautifully trained sheltie, son. Congratulations!"

David thanked her and moved back to his place in the line. He knew he was beaming like an idiot, but he couldn't help himself. 199½! That was the highest score he had ever received!

Johnny and Mr. Martz were waiting to pound him on the back when he filed out of the ring with the other handlers. Mr. Martz seemed as pleased as if his own son had won the trophy. "Flash will probably refuse to ride with Shad going home tonight," he declared.

They watched the conclusion of the judging in the other ring; then during the lunch break they headed for the Martz car. David looked around for Bert Norman but did not see the youngster. Rain was falling as they crossed the large parking area.

"Bet we'll see snow before morning," Johnny said, hunching his shoulders.

Mr. Martz grunted. "I may wish I'd put the snow tires on."

"Boy, I hope we don't get stuck somewhere," David said. "Dad will have a fit if I'm not home in time to go to school in the morning."

They ate a leisurely lunch. Johnny and Shad were not due to appear in the ring until around three. When they arrived back at the trial, the building was buzzing with excited talk. Word had come that a private aircraft carrying the top show-winning German shepherd dog in the nation was overdue and feared down.

"Hey, Montana!"

David looked up. The voice belonged to the same member of the Idaho Falls club who had hailed him that morning. The man wasn't smiling now. "You're from Winnegar, Montana, aren't you?" he asked.

"Yes, we all three are," David replied.

"They think the plane must be down somewhere in your area. It landed at Billings last night, and the pilot was warned that a bad storm was moving in. He took off right away trying to beat the storm. The last radio contact was at Winnegar."

"Who was in the plane?" Mr. Martz asked.

"Price Sargent, the pilot, and two others."

Mr. Martz looked blank. "Am I supposed to know who Price Sargent is?"

"Sargent is one of the top professional dog handlers in the business," the Idaho Falls man said. "He's kennel manager for Walter Eton. You've surely heard of Etonhill Kennels. Etonhill Princess Tanya, the dog that's supposed to be on the plane, has won more Best in Shows and more Groups in the past two years than any other German shepherd."

"Lot of rough country around Winnegar," Mr. Martz observed.

"They say the pilot was experienced, but he must have been crazy to head into weather like that. You've had four inches of snow over there since morning."

Mr. Martz shook his head. "Bad business this time of year."

They found a place to sit and watch the Novice A dogs work. These were Johnny and Shad's competition. Some of them performed very well, but David saw none that he would score as high as Flash. The Novice exercises were simple compared to those in Open, and yet Johnny spoke for many others when he said, "I don't care about a trophy; I just want my leg."

There were twenty-two dogs entered in Novice A, and Johnny's name was well down the list. He was still waiting to go into the ring when a disturbance erupted outside the building. "It's that big mongrel again!" David heard someone say.

"Where's the dogcatcher?" a woman demanded. "I thought there weren't supposed to be any loose dogs in the park and particularly not down here at the show grounds!"

"I know what I'd do," said a contestant from Utah. "I'd

shoot the sucker. He tackled that collie this morning, and he was back again at noon. Somebody's going to get bitten."

David and Johnny hurried to look, but the big dog had already been driven off. "I wish you could see him," Johnny said. "He's a big skinny brown dog. Doesn't look as if he's had a meal in a week."

They went back to watch the obedience, and finally the ring steward beckoned to Johnny. The tall, redheaded boy had no more than entered the ring when young Bert Norman turned up. "Can we take Flash for a walk now?"

"Why don't you wait a few minutes?" David suggested. "I want to watch Johnny and Shad."

Bert had two friends with him. "Flash is going to get the trophy for being the smartest dog in the whole show," he announced importantly. "Couldn't I take him, David?"

"You'd better wait," David told him. Flash would not enjoy being led around by the youngster, and besides, David didn't much like handing his dog over to a stranger.

"But my mother says we have to go. Please, David. Just let me lead him around a little bit. I'll just take him up and down the sidewalk."

David debated. He had sort of promised. He looked and saw that Johnny had already begun. "Well, okay," he said.

He showed the youngster how to handle the leash and made him promise that he would positively be back inside the building in ten minutes. Flash tossed him a reproachful look, but moved off obediently with the three small boys.

In the ring Shad ambled through his paces with bored proficiency. At best he was not an eager worker, and the day had been long. Dogs and handlers and judges—all were beginning to grow weary. "I don't think," said Mr. Martz with wry humor, "that you need worry about Shad beating Flash out for High Score in Trial."

"He'll pass, though," David replied. "He'll get his leg without any trouble, and that's more than a lot of these dogs are doing."

Johnny had just finished when people inside the building became aware of a commotion outside. Suddenly the door was thrust open and a youngster plunged into the room screaming hysterically, "He's eating him! That big dog's chewing up the little one!"

David swiveled in his seat. Dread shot through him as he recognized one of the small boys who had been with Bert. The youngster's eyes were two round black dots of horror in a face devoid of color. David jumped to his feet. Heedless of the folding chair collapsing with a bang behind him, he plunged through the staring spectators. "Where's Flash?" he demanded. "Where's . . . ?"

The boy was not able to talk. David broke off and started for the door. A man barred his path. "If that sheltie out there was yours, son, you're too late."

2.

Dude in the Saddle

The road home from Idaho Falls seemed endless. Mr. Martz was driving and Johnny rode up front with him. For the last fifty miles they had hardly spoken to each other. David sat in the back seat with Shad and two trophies he could scarcely bear to look at. He took scant comfort from the knowledge that his dog had died a hero. Young Bert had tried to drive away the savage mongrel and in doing so had drawn the brute's ferocity to himself. Flash had defended the boy, but hampered by the leash, he had not been able to elude the punishing jaws. Police had shot the mongrel, and Mr. Martz had wrapped the sheltie in a plastic ground cloth and laid him in the trunk of the car.

Not wanting to think, David stared out the window into the black, stormy night. Hot tears flooded his eyes. He had won the trial and lost his dog.

They put chains on going into West Yellowstone, Montana, but before they came to Bozeman, they ran out of the storm. When finally they arrived in Winnegar at two in the morning, stars shown above a white, still landscape.

"If you're going to bury Flash tonight, I'll help you," Johnny offered as the car stopped in front of the Hollis home on Thorburn Street.

David shook his head. Then, aware that his friend probably could not see the movement in the dark, he said, "I'll take care of him."

He caught the glint of the trophies—the small one from Open A and the big twenty-four-inch cup he had won for High Score in Trial. Because a sheltie had won, the club officials had put a sheltie figurine on top. Suddenly overcome, he blurted, "You can bury the trophies. I don't want them. I don't want to see them ever."

"I'll take care of them," Johnny replied softly.

Mr. Martz got out of the car to open the trunk. He laid his hand on David's shoulder as David lifted the plastic-wrapped bundle. Neither of them spoke. David wanted to express his thanks for the ride, but the muscles of his mouth were twisted so that he couldn't speak. Blindly he stumbled up the front walk toward the house. He didn't even say good night.

A light had been left on for him in the living room, but he walked around the house. Snow sifted into his shoes. He felt the icy wetness seeping through his socks but didn't care. He didn't care if he got pneumonia.

Tenderly he set his burden down. He tried the small door to the garage and, finding it unlocked, he pushed inside. By touch he located a shovel. He knew exactly where he would bury Flash. In the summertime the sheltie liked to lie in the shade by the back step. A rain spout kept the earth damp, and Flash had worn a hollow to fit his body.

The earth under the snow was not frozen. Until this storm, Winnegar had seen no winter weather. David began to dig, and in the starlight the black mound of dirt on top of the snow grew swiftly.

Suddenly an oblong of light slashed across the yard. David looked up and realized that someone had come into the kitchen. Almost immediately another light flared on the enclosed back porch. David could hear the heavy shuffling of his father's bedroom slippers on the bare floor, and a moment later the bolt-type lock clattered.

"That you out there, David?" Marshall Hollis queried.

"Yeah."

The door swung wide, and Dad in his bathrobe loomed a black bulk against the light. "I thought I heard you come home. What are you doing?"

"Burying my dog," David mumbled.

"What?"

"I'm burying my dog!" David snapped, his voice sharp with impatience. He knew he had no right to be uncivil, but he was tired and sick with grief.

For a wonder Dad hung on to his temper. "What happened?" he asked gently.

David didn't look up from his digging. "Another dog got him. A big stray."

For a long time Marshall Hollis stood without speaking. Finally he said, "It's almost two-thirty. Can't that wait until tomorrow?"

"No," David answered curtly.

His father stood a while longer, and finally he said, "You ought to get some gloves and put on your overshoes."

David ignored him, nor caring that his own hurt should hurt another. He did not look up when his father closed the door and shuffled back inside.

The tears came again as David finished the grave and laid Flash, still wrapped in the plastic ground cloth, in it. Scarcely able to see, he shoveled the dirt back into the hole.

When he went in the house, his mother was sitting at the kitchen table in her housecoat, her hair done up on rollers. The smell of hot chocolate filled the room. "I've made some cocoa, David," she said. "I'm awfully sorry to hear about Flash."

He drew a long breath. He knew he couldn't talk without his voice breaking. "You shouldn't have got up, Mom. I don't want anything, thanks."

He fled to the room he shared with his twelve-year-old brother. Harvey was asleep and he tried not to wake him. In darkness he shed his clothes and climbed into bed, wincing as the springs creaked. At once Harvey stirred. "David?" a small sleepy voice queried.

David didn't answer.

Harvey turned over, and David hoped the younger boy would sink back into slumber, but suddenly a small light flared at the head of Harvey's bed. "I thought I heard you," the youngster said.

"I don't want to talk," David told him. "It's three in the morning."

Harvey sat up. "How'd you do at the dog show?"

"It wasn't a dog show. It was an obedience trial. And I did lousy. Turn out the light."

"You don't have to bite my head off!"

Harvey flopped back down and punched the light switch. As the room was plunged again into darkness, David knew that he ought to apologize, but he didn't. He lay still and pulled his sorrow about him.

The ringing of the telephone awakened him. He opened his eyes and realized that day had come. The ringing stopped and he could hear the low murmur of his mother's voice. He looked to see the time, but the clock on a chair beside his bed had stopped. He had not thought to wind it. Harvey's bed was empty.

"Somebody should have called me," he muttered, throwing back his covers.

"David! David! Telephone!"

Barefoot and yawning, he padded into the living room and over to the phone on his mother's writing desk. His father and brother were already seated at the kitchen dinette. He smelled bacon and waffles.

As soon as he spoke, Johnny's voice crackled excitedly over the wire. "Hey, David, you know that plane that was missing? Link just called me. It cracked up on my uncle's place. A search plane spotted it last night, and Uncle Tom took a rescue party up there. They just got back a little while ago."

Jolted wide awake, David said, "How bad was it?"

"Link says nobody got killed. There were four of them. Only the pilot and one other guy were hurt badly enough to go to the hospital."

David ran his fingers through his hair. "What about the dog? Did Link say anything about Etonhill Princess Tanya?"

"She's what I called about," Johnny said. "She's disappeared. She was in a crate, and the crate broke open when the plane crashed. Everybody was knocked unconscious, I guess, or anyway they were too busy worrying about each other to think of her right away. When they got to checking, she was gone. Price Sargent told Link he'd give him a hundred dollars if he'd find her."

David whistled. "That's a nice piece of change."

"That's what I thought," Johnny agreed. "Link wants us

to come out after school and help him. He'll have some horses all saddled. We can ride up to the plane and take a look around."

Link was Johnny's thirteen-year-old cousin, a son of Tom Ittlesby. Perhaps because he was a country boy who had been given responsibility and taught self-reliance, he had always seemed closer in age to Johnny and David than to Harvey.

"Aunt Elsie's coming to town this afternoon to do some shopping," Johnny continued. "She'll give us a ride out, and Dad says he'll come get us. I figure we can skip seventh-period study hall and be out there by three-thirty."

David grunted in agreement. "When does Link get out of school?" Johnny's cousin, he knew, attended the country school a quarter-mile up the road from his dad's ranch home.

"He doesn't have school. The wind blew a tree down on the schoolhouse roof last night, and they're fixing it today."

They concluded their conversation, and David raced to get dressed for school. His mother had his plate ready when he hurried to the table. "What's all the excitement?" she asked.

Between mouthfuls of waffle and hot syrup he related what he knew about the plane crash. "Price Sargent told Link he'd pay him at least a hundred dollars to get Etonhill Princess Tanya back. We're going to split it three ways."

"Wow!" exclaimed Harvey.

"It gets dark before seven," objected Dad. "You won't have much time."

"We're going to skip seventh-period study hall," David said.

"I would think," Dad remarked, "that after last night you'd be ready to give up this foolishness over dogs."

"Aw, Dad!" The thought of Flash made the food stick in David's throat. He felt tears well in his eyes and could not stop them. Angrily he slammed down his napkin and stalked from the table. Why couldn't his father be even a little bit like Johnny Martz' dad?

At ten minutes to three that afternoon, when the boys walked out of the high school, the sun was shining and the snow melting. "It'll be colder up in the mountains than it is here," Johnny warned. "Better dress warm."

They arrived at the ranch at twenty minutes after the hour. Link Ittlesby, wearing chaps and a cowboy hat, had three horses saddled and waiting.

"Hi, fellas! Hurry up!" he greeted them. "Mr. Sargent just called Pa. They've had a plane up all day looking for Tanya—that's what they call her—and haven't been able to spot her. They're raising the reward to five hundred dollars!"

"FIVE HUNDRED DOLLARS!" David and Johnny echoed in chorus. "Man, what I . . ." Johnny began.

"Let's go! Let's get a gittin'," Link interrupted. "We've only got about three hours before dark!"

Johnny mounted first. While Link adjusted stirrups for him, David climbed awkwardly aboard a fat stocking-legged red horse. Shorty was the slowest horse on the ranch, he knew from past experience, but the big sorrel was gentle. David had ridden less than a dozen times in his life, and he had no yearning to try a livelier mount.

When they were ready to go, Link led off at a gallop up

the snowy draw. At his pony's heels raced a black-and-white farm collie. David watched the dog and felt a knife stab in his heart, but his mind was swiftly taken up with the physical demands of the occasion. Link rode as if he were glued to his saddle. Even Johnny managed to look fairly competent, but David had to hold on for dear life.

Half a mile from the ranch buildings, the draw narrowed abruptly. Link pulled to a walk and took the lead up a cattle trail that wound along a small creek. "It'll take us over an hour to get up there," he called over his shoulder. "We won't have too much time to look around. Pa thinks the dog is either dead or she's hiding right close. He says she was probably spooked by the crash, but when she gets hungry, she'll come looking for the people she was with."

"Couldn't they tell from her tracks whether she was hurt?" Johnny asked.

David had wondered the same thing. Jouncing along in the rear, though, he had difficulty keeping up with the conversation. Shorty refused to move out on a walk like the other horses. He would poke and poke, then trot to catch up.

"The snow covered up everything," Link said. "After the snowmobiles got down to the ranch this morning, Dad and the sheriff went back up with horses to pack out those guys' stuff. They didn't find any dog tracks at all."

"How come they took horses?" Johnny demanded, "when they had snowmobiles?"

"Because," his cousin explained, "the snow isn't hardly deep enough to cover the rocks, and it was beginning to thaw."

They followed the trail made by the pack string. It led

them to a gate in a barbed-wire fence, then climbed stead-ily through rugged range country used only for summer grazing. At every level stretch Link would push his mount into a gallop. David tried to imitate the way the ranch boy rode, but he soon developed sores from rubbing against the saddle. He hated to say anything, though, and let the kid think that town boys were sissies.

As the sun dropped toward the horizon, gray clouds piled up in the north. "It's going to snow some more," Link predicted.

A chill breeze sprang up. Johnny held a mittened hand over his nose. "Is it just me, or is it getting colder? How much farther, Link?"

"About half a mile. Well, no, it's farther than that. It's about half a mile as the crow flies, but these crowbaits don't fly."

The youngster laughed at his joke, but David failed to appreciate the humor. His knees were beginning to ache as if someone had driven spikes through them. He felt as though he had sat for two days with his legs bent in the same position.

"You know what I'm going to do with my share of the reward money?" Johnny said. "I'm going to buy a car."

David cocked one eyebrow. "What's one-third of noth-ing?" he called. "We haven't found this dog yet."

He, of course, would buy another sheltie. A third of five hundred dollars plus what he had in his savings would buy a better-bred dog than Flash had been.

"Hey, what's this?" Johnny exclaimed, reining up sud-denly to point at the ground. "Aren't these dog tracks in the snow?"

Link turned his mount around and rode back.

"They're dog tracks, all right," David affirmed.

"They're Skipper's tracks," Link stated flatly. "My dog made 'em."

No, David thought. Link probably didn't want to admit that he had ridden right past without noticing, but these footprints had not been made by the ranch dog. Skipper had a lot of hair between the toes of his splay feet, and he had big dewclaws on his hind feet. These tracks had been made by clean, closely knit feet.

Eager for any excuse to dismount, David swung clumsily from his saddle. His cramped legs caved unexpectedly and he gasped in surprise.

"Boy, what have you been drinking?" Johnny jeered.

David grinned sheepishly, then laughed outright as his friend swung down and stood swaying before gingerly taking a step.

"Bunch of dudes!" Link hooted.

Together they bent to study the tracks in the snow. Beyond all doubt, the prints had been made by a large, short-coated dog. "They're fairly fresh, too," Johnny pointed out. "If they'd been made while it was still thawing, they'd be sort of blurry."

"What are we waiting for?" Link exclaimed.

David groaned as he climbed stiffly back into his saddle. "Maybe you cowboy types had better go ahead without me," he suggested. "I can't ride as fast as you can, and it's going to be dark soon. I think I'd rather go on up to see the plane."

"Aw, come on, David," Johnny urged.

David shook his head. "My legs are rubbed raw. I'd

only hold you back. Besides—" he grinned smugly "—if Link's dad is right, I may find Tanya waiting by the plane."

Although Johnny protested, Link saw no harm in splitting up. "He can't get lost," he insisted. "All he's got to do is follow the trail made by the pack string this morning. And if he does get off somehow, all he has to do is stay in the saddle. Ol' Shorty will bring him straight home."

"Yeah, but what if we follow this track for miles and miles?" Johnny argued.

"Well, we'll come back," Link said. "David can wait by the plane until we come. Come on, if we sit here yakking all day, nobody'll have time to go anywhere."

Reluctantly, Johnny gave in. "Wish you'd change your mind," he said to David.

"Don't worry, I'll share the reward money if I find Tanya," David replied airily.

Shorty objected to proceeding alone, but when Johnny and Link rode out of sight, David finally got him lined out. In spite of the fact that the big sorrel's slow walk didn't cover much ground, David didn't crowd him. Anything was better than a trot.

Link's estimate of the distance to the wrecked plane proved to be little better than a wild guess. David rode what he judged to be half a mile and came to a gate. He went through and rode another half-mile, and still the trail wound on. By then the sun had dropped behind the hills, and the cold was beginning to find its way into David's fingers and toes. He speculated that somehow or other he had gotten on the wrong path; yet he knew he couldn't have. There had been no other beaten trail.

He kept going, aware suddenly of flecks of moisture in

the air. What would he do, he wondered uneasily, if snow covered up the tracks of the pack string?

On the verge of becoming genuinely concerned, he remembered that Link had said he need not worry about getting lost. His horse would know in which direction home lay. David patted the sorrel's shoulder. "I hope you've been paying attention, buddy."

Ten minutes later he spied the plane. The red and silver four-seater had clipped the tops off a grove of aspens, slid on its belly across a sagebrush-covered clearing, and finally flipped up on its nose at the foot of a giant fur tree.

Although Shorty had probably been one of the pack string that morning, David could not get him within thirty feet of the wreck. He snorted and jumped around like a bronc. In disgust, David dismounted and looked for something to tie the horse to. His gaze settled on a weathered juniper snag. Very likely Shorty was trained to stand ground-tied, but David feared to take a chance.

The plane had crashed in a shallow gully between two low ridges. Had it remained air-borne another three hundred feet, it would have smashed into dense timber on the face of a mountain. Looking at the battered, perpendicular fuselage, David marveled that any of its passengers had managed to survive. Curious, he stepped closer to look inside. The windshield and side windows were shattered; one door was off.

What he saw surprised him. He had forgotten that Link's dad and the sheriff had collected all cargo and personal belongings. Seat belts dangled and seat cushions had dropped forward, but everything else, even the dog crate—probably one of the collapsible variety—was gone.

He spied reddish-brown stains on the instrument panel, and there was a pool of frozen blood by the rudder pedals. A few black hairs caught in the ruptured door hinge was the only evidence that a dog had been included among the craft's passengers.

Thoughtfully, David turned from his inspection of the interior. If Mr. Ittlesby's theory were correct, Tanya might have returned. He might be able to discover some tracks. When he stepped away from the big tree, however, his heel slipped on a gnarled root and threw him with a thump against the wing of the plane. He grunted and fell down.

Startled by the sudden commotion, Shorty flew back on his bridle reins and jerked the juniper snag loose. As it leaped at him, he whistled in terror and reared. David shouted and scrambled to his feet, but he was too late. Shorty plunged sideways and bolted with the dry stump lurching and snatching at his heels.

David stared after his stampeding mount in dismay. Belatedly, he realized that he should have made certain before he tied the horse that the old juniper was solidly anchored. For a minute, as he became aware of the settling dusk and realized that he was alone and afoot, he shared Shorty's panic. On the run, he started after the horse.

Shorty, pursued by the snag, had angled sharply up a ridge. David progressed less than a hundred yards before he decided that running uphill through snow, wearing heavy overshoes, was different from making a couple of quick laps around the high school athletic field. He slowed to a trot, then to a walk. By the time he reached the top of the ridge, his lungs ached from the inrush of frigid air. Bracing himself against the wind, he paused to catch his breath. Shorty had vanished.

"Old crowbait!" he muttered.

He heard a rifle shot then. It seemed close, but he couldn't be sure. The wind and the thickening clouds distorted sound. He wondered who would be shooting. Neither Johnny nor Link had brought along a gun. What had been the target? Hunting season wouldn't open for another three weeks.

David shrugged. He had a more immediate problem. Although he couldn't spot Shorty, he could easily follow the trail of the dragging juniper snag. Accordingly, he broke into a trot, heading downhill now. Tiny crystals of snow stung his face, but at least his hands and feet were no longer cold.

In the gathering dusk he almost failed to recognize the juniper snag when he came to it. He was right beside it when he saw the broken ends of the reins dangling from the twisted wood. Again he stopped to catch his breath. This was good, he thought. Freed of the snag that had terrified him, Shorty probably wouldn't run much farther.

With renewed hope he started on. He knew he must hurry and get back to the plane. If Link and Johnny arrived at the crash site before he returned, they wouldn't know what to think.

As the minutes passed, though, Shorty's tracks became increasingly more difficult to follow. Trails of other horses or cattle crisscrossed the area. In the deepening darkness, the white bulks of treeless nearer ridges stood out against the black mass of the mountains, but holes and bushes and rocks and tracks all began to look alike.

Doubt began to nag at David. He stopped repeatedly to

bend low and peer at the depressions in the snow. Finally he knew he had lost the trail. He had run out of any kind of tracks!

Panic stirring in him, he quartered back along his own trail. He must have missed where Shorty turned off. Nothing to worry about, actually, he reassured himself. If worse came to worse, he could simply follow his own tracks back to the plane. He could ride double with one of the other boys. Shorty would undoubtedly circle and they'd find him waiting down at the first gate.

Even with the full blackness of night, the snow reflected enough light so that he could see to walk. Then he began to worry about the length of time he had been away from the wrecked plane. What if his friends rode to the crash site, discovered him gone, and struck out immediately for home?

He halted to study for a moment a ridge he had descended earlier. He could angle around its lower edge, he figured, and strike the pack-string trail below the wrecked plane. "Be less chance of missing those guys," he said aloud.

Accordingly, he abandoned his own back trail. As he tramped confidently around the point of the ridge, he actually felt pleased with himself that he could make a levelheaded decision in a situation that might shake up a lot of town kids. The gully on the other side seemed deeper than he remembered, but this discovery did not disturb him. When he was riding, he hadn't paid much attention to the sheltering ridges.

Gradually the darkness became more intense, and presently he noticed that the snow was falling in bigger flakes. His legs told him when he struck the bottom of the draw.

Tensely he strained to see the trail. "There!" he exclaimed, and knew a sudden shame at his feeling of relief.

But it wasn't the trail. It was a tiny stream. Ice cracked beneath his weight and mud sucked at his overshoes. He didn't get wet—the water couldn't have been more than a couple of inches deep—but the realization of his mistake jarred him.

He couldn't remember a creek in the hollow where the plane had crashed! Aware that his heart had begun to pound, he turned up the draw. He must have come in below the trail made by the pack string. He tried to remember how the country had looked. He scarcely knew that he was hurrying until his lungs began to wheeze in protest.

He lost track of time. He walked until he came to the lower fringe of timber on the big mountain and then he knew for sure that he was in the wrong place. He climbed a ridge and dropped into the next hollow. Here he thought he spied the plane, but when he drew close he found a huge old dead snag leaning against another tree.

"I'm lost," he said, and was steadied by the sound of his own voice.

He stood still, breathing deeply, trying to think. "Oh, Stupid!" he exclaimed. Why hadn't he yelled for help?

Filling his lungs, he cupped his hands to make a megaphone. "Hel-lo!" he called.

The wind answered him. It spoke among the trees in mocking stage whispers. It snickered across the snow. Frightened, he turned and shouted again, his voice rising with despair. Then he tensed, as from the darkness below him an unfamiliar masculine voice bellowed in reply. "Hal-lo!"

Joyously he replied. With a tremendous sense of relief he began to stride downhill. Whoever the man might be, the sight of him would be more welcome than the promise of half a dozen checks for the return of Etonhill Princess Tanya.

Twice within a hundred yards he stopped to call, and each time the voice answered promptly. Finally, in the gloom ahead, a movement caught his eye. A dog, he thought, straining to see. No, whatever it was, it was too large for a dog.

An odd chill stole across him. The dark shape humping toward him looked like a bear! "Hi!" he called sharply.

"Yah!" came the immediate response.

The dark form was not a bear, but a man bent over. What manner of man, David wondered with prickling fear, would travel about on all fours!

3.

The Cabin in Bootleggers' Ravine

David shuddered. Fear quivered in him as he strained to see better the oddly contorted shape that moved toward him through the snow-whipped darkness. He did not believe in werewolves or other manner of nonhuman beings, but a lifetime addiction to horror movies had conditioned him to think of such things. These hills that had lain glistening in the sun and beckoning by day were turned suddenly hostile and sinister by night.

As the apparition shuffled slowly closer, David fought panic. Then at a distance of perhaps twenty yards, the thing halted. As it drew itself erect, its appearance changed abruptly from animal form to human.

"Hallo! I am startle you, yah?"

The man spoke with an accent, but there was nothing otherworldly about his voice. David found his tongue and regained control of his motor impulses at the same time. He moved forward. "Hi. Are you lost, too?"

"Lost? No, I'm not lost. I am twist my ankle, though."

The man was very small. When they stood side by side, the top of the stranger's head came barely to David's shoulder. A huge sheepskin coat dwarfed the small frame it encompassed.

"You are lost, eh?"

David nodded. "My horse got away from me. I was looking at that wrecked plane."

"Plane? So that was it. I hear the snow machines this

morning and all day a small plane is flying. But that was south of here."

"I guess I'm pretty stupid," David said.

"Maybe, but you don't panic. You yell 'hallo' instead of 'halp.'"

"I was getting scared, though," David admitted. "Believe me, I was pretty glad to hear your voice."

"Well, my cabin is close, but I am travel pretty slow. I am like lame dog on my two hands and good leg."

"I bet I could carry you piggy-back," David said impulsively.

The little man caught hold of David's arm. "You are strong boy, but old Heinie makes pretty much burden."

"Let me try it," David urged. "I can set you down when I get tired. Do you think you can direct me?"

"Yah, I am know this country. All right, we try it. I cook a fine supper when we get home."

David knelt so that the little man could climb onto his back and was amazed as he lurched to his feet that any adult could weigh so little. Surely the great sheepskin coat must account for a fourth of the total pounds. "Where to?" he asked.

"Up this low ridge. You will strike a trail by that big pine tree."

David wondered if the old man could actually see the tree. He hated to admit his own blindness. "Tell me if I get off course," he said. "I have to watch where I'm putting my feet."

The grade rose gradually enough, so that the going was not too difficult even with the snow, but he found he had to adjust to the unaccustomed weight. Not having his hands free made considerable difference in his balance.

"You are living near here, son?"

David paused to catch his breath. "No, I live in town. My best friend is a nephew of Tom Ittlesby. My name is David Hollis."

"Ah," said the old man, "I know Lincoln Ittlesby. He is a nice boy. He comes to see old Heinie sometimes."

"Do you have a ranch, Mr. Heinie?"

The little man chuckled. "Mr. Heinie Wehring is having nothing. Since I retire from Yellowstone Park I am looking for uranium."

"You're a prospector?"

"A prospector, yah."

David started climbing again. As he trudged along, he debated telling the old man about Etonhill Princess Tanya. Since Heinie Wehring lived in the vicinity of the plane crash, he might be the logical one to find the dog. He could probably make good use of the reward money, too.

On the crest of the ridge they came to a towering pine tree that stood like a sentinel apart from the timber that mantled the upper slopes of the mountain. Barely discernible in the snow was a stock trail. "Now, to the left," the old man said. "By that big boulder. I left my rifle there."

"Your rifle?" David repeated in surprise. Then he remembered that he had heard a shot. "You didn't shoot a dog, did you?" he asked in sudden alarm.

"A dog? No, I have seen no dog. Did you lose a dog?"

"Not exactly."

David spied the weapon, but instead of picking it up, he leaned against the rock to unload his passenger. "Got to rest a minute."

The old prospector hobbled painfully to the rifle. Working the bolt, he pointed the muzzle to the sky and pulled the trigger on the empty chamber. "There. We know it is unloaded. Why do you think I shoot a dog?"

David decided to tell him. Although Johnny and Link had designs on the reward money, he thought Heinie Wehring had better know the whole story so that he would appreciate Tanya's value. In spite of the fact that real wolves hadn't been known in southcentral Montana for fifty years, a German shepherd dog roaming free in the mountains might very easily be mistaken for a wolf.

"Ah, you were looking for the dog, then," the old man exclaimed.

"Yes. Link and Johnny and I were going to split the reward if we found her."

"How you came to be separated from your friends?"

David explained about his saddle sores. "Those other guys are lots better riders than I am, and they wanted to follow Tanya's tracks. I was supposed to wait by the wrecked plane, but my horse broke loose. I thought I could catch him."

"Lincoln and Johnny meant to join you at the plane?"

"Yeah, that was the plan."

"Hmm. They probably are giving you up and have gone on home. If my telephone is working, we will call to say you are all right."

"Do you have a telephone up here on the mountain?" David asked in surprise.

"Yah, a telephone. I can call the Wilson ranch if a tree has not blown down across the line."

The little man climbed aboard again, and they started along the trail. With the added burden of the rifle, David found he had all the load he could manage. He began to realize, too, that he had done considerable tramping since Shorty had bolted from the scene of the crashed plane.

The trail led through scattered timber, wound across an open shoulder of the mountain, and finally dived into a narrow ravine. David began to think he would never last to the old man's cabin. "I guess I'll have to put you down again, Mr. Wehring," he said.

"Thirty yards more and we are here," said the prospector. "And I am not Mr. Wehring. I am Heinie."

At that instant a chorus of yelping and howling and barking such as David had never heard before burst on the night silence. "What is *that?*" he exclaimed, halting to listen.

"Our brother the coyote."

"Must be a bunch of them," David observed.

"No, he is just one."

As he stood, thrilled by the pulsating song, David spotted the black shape of a small building among the trees. He moved forward, his footsteps crisp in the snow here in the silence of the ravine. Heinie's cabin was not much larger than the Hollis garage. Its windows glinted dully in the darkness.

With care David set the old man down. Apparently there was a rock there that served for a doorstep, because all at once Heinie seemed taller. A latch clattered, then hinges creaked as the door swung inward. "Come in. Don't bump your head. The door is low. I'll make a light."

Warm air that smelled of fried food smote David's nostrils. Unable to see, he felt his way inside, located the door, and pushed it shut. Heinie moved in the blackness in front of him, his footsteps halting on the bare wood floor. Presently a match scraped and flared. As the old man lighted a coal-oil lamp sitting on a table in the middle of the room, the contents of the cabin leaped into focus. David blinked in surprise to see a modern refrigerator. It seemed out of place with the massive, old-fashioned wood range, the primitive sink with a hand pump, and the coal-oil lamp. "But . . ." he stammered, "do you have electricity?"

Heinie's wizened face, framed by the collar of the huge sheepskin coat, was gnome-like in the soft glow of the lamp. "The icebox? It uses bottled gas. That is my one luxury."

Curiously, David looked about the single room. The kitchen was at one end. Built-in bunk beds with stacks of old newspapers stored underneath dominated the other end. Three straight chairs were ranged around the square, hand-hewn table. On a small lowboy behind the door was a transistor radio and another piece of equipment that looked like something a small boy might construct from materials obtained at the city dump.

"You are impressed with my telephone?" Heinie asked, amused.

David turned his attention once more to his host. The prospector had removed his cap and exposed a sparse covering of unkempt grizzled hair. His deeply lined face was the face of an old, old man. Somehow David had not expected him to be so old. "Uh," he fumbled, "is that really a telephone? Does it work?"

"Yah, sure. You know the history of that phone? In Prohibition this cabin belonged to moonshiners. There was a still up above. This ravine today is called Bootleggers' Ravine."

"They made bootleg whisky?" David asked, intrigued.

"Yah. When the law-enforcement officers would come, the man who lived on Mr. Wilson's ranch at that time would phone a warning."

"And this is that same phone?"

"Yah. I think the ladies who make the shopkeeper of antiques rich would like it very much, yah?"

David grinned. "My own mother would give her right arm to get hold of something like that phone."

"You don't tell her then, Davy, hah?"

"No, I won't tell her, Heinie.

The little man shrugged off his sheepskin coat and hobbled over to the strange-looking contraption. "I'll call Mr. Wilson. He can call Mr. Ittlesby on the public telephone."

Pulling a chair over for himself, he indicated for David to sit, and turned his attention to the telephone. At the base of the antique instrument was a lever about three inches long. Heinie pumped this back and forth to produce a raucous ringing that sounded like an alarm clock with a bad cold. "They should be home. They are always home in the evening because they have small children who go to school."

They waited. In less than thirty seconds David heard a voice crackle over the wire. "Hallo!" said Heinie. ". . . Oh, fine! Everything's fine. And how's yourself. . . ? I have a favor to ask . . . Yah, a favor. I have as my guest—what is your name, Davy?"

"Hollis," supplied David.

"Mr. Wilson, his name is David Hollis . . . Hollis, yah. He got separated from his companions, but he is fine . . . He is ALL RIGHT."

The little prospector frowned as static crackled over the line. "When the wind blows, it is bad," he said to David.

"Mr. Wilson, will you call Mr. Ittlesby . . . ? Will you call
. . . yah, Tom Ittlesby . . . Yah, and tell him the boy is all
right. He is with me . . . Yah. Thank you . . . Good night!"

The telephone squawked as he hung up. "So, Davy, it is
done. I will light the gas lantern, which gives a better
light. Then I'll build up the fire, and soon it is warm. You
are hungry?"

"I could eat a horse!"

Heinie smiled. "How about fresh deer liver?"

"*Fresh* deer liver?" David repeated. Of course! He
should have guessed. A man didn't carry a rifle in a snowstorm to kill rattlesnakes!

The old man stepped to his coat and pulled a plastic-
wrapped bundle from a pocket. David could see the deep
red of the raw liver. Heinie glanced at him. "Is it so bad,
Davy? The bow season is open. A man with a bow and
arrows may go out and kill a deer. Is the deer more dead
because I use a rifle?"

David scarcely knew what to say. Game laws—all laws
—were made to be obeyed. He had been brought up that
way.

"I shock you. I am sorry, but I am not sorry for the
deer. Old Heinie does not waste one bite. In the morning I
will bring the deer home. I do not let one bite spoil. I
don't shoot a trophy and waste the meat."

"I guess it's none of my business," David said, aware
that he sounded stuffy.

Heinie pointed with his finger for emphasis. "Wasted
meat is everybody's business, but I eat what I kill." He
smiled suddenly. "I am a poacher, though, hah? Davy,
poached meat tastes the best!"

"Shouldn't we do something about your ankle, Heinie, before we think about eating?" David suggested, anxious to change the subject.

"No, first we eat. A sprain' ankle I can have any time. Company for dinner is a seldom thing."

David was amazed at how swiftly the big range heated the room. Within five minutes he shed his jacket. He offered to assist with the preparations for supper, but the old man would have no help. He dropped a glob of grease into an iron skillet and set it on the stove. Then he sliced a large onion and peeled and sliced two potatoes and dumped all three into the skillet. When the aroma of good food cooking filled the cabin, he got out another skillet and laid strips of bacon to fry. Swiftly and expertly he cut and trimmed slices of the deer liver. When that too was frying, he turned to David. "You drink coffee? Tea? I have canned milk."

David preferred milk with his meals, but not condensed milk. "Water will be just fine, thanks."

When Heinie set the meal on the table, he dug into his pocket and pulled out a silver watch. "Nine-forty. A little late, even for society. Let's eat, Davy."

Although he had always thought he did not care much for liver, David tried the hot, fresh venison liver. To his surprise, eaten along with bites of crisp bacon, it was delicious. So were the well-seasoned potatoes and onions. Of course he had worked up a considerable appetite—he was almost hungry enough to eat hoofs and horns—but truly Heinie had engineered a feast.

"This is the best chow I've eaten in a month!" he told the beaming prospector.

"I will send you home some venison steaks," said Heinie.

"Oh, no! Dad would have a fit if he knew the deer had been poached."

"Too bad. Too bad," Heinie sympathized.

For dessert they ate canned peaches. When David finally pushed away from the table, a vast sense of comfort and contentment overtook him. "You know, Heinie," he said, yawning, "I think you've got it made. You have a house and you're warm and you've got food, and you can do just as you please."

"Everything I have, but one," agreed the little prospector.

"What's that?"

"I am no longer young. The world belongs to the young. I am an old man who will be dead one day, and no one will notice even that I am gone."

"You're not so old," David protested.

Heinie smiled. "Some days a hundred and ten. My health is not good. I lose weight in spite of all I eat. But, here—" he spread his hands "—let's you and me talk about other things. It's been a long time since I have someone to visit me."

The prospector, it developed, had for many years before his retirement been winter keeper at various locations in Yellowstone National Park. While David washed dishes, he soaked his swollen ankle in a tub of hot water and told of his encounters with the animal denizens of his often inaccessible but never lonesome world.

David thought the sprained ankle looked bad, but the old man did not seem to be alarmed. "In the bottom drawer of the bureau is an elastic bandage. This ankle does this. I wrap it up for a week or two, and it is all right."

For the night David kicked off his shoes and climbed fully clad into the top bunk. Heinie had only one spare blanket. The old man crawled into the lower bunk, and as David watched the gas light fade slowly into darkness, he wondered what his father would say about his missing school in the morning. Then he knew no more until he awakened to see daylight streaming in through the windows.

The cabin seemed warm. He raised up on one elbow, his head only a few inches from the rough boards of the sloping roof. Heinie stood at the table stirring some kind of batter.

"Ah, Davy, you wake up! You are liking some pancakes for breakfast?"

"Morning, Heinie. Sure, I like pancakes. How's the ankle?"

"Not too bad. Maybe, though, I impose on my young friend if he lets me."

"Sure," David said, climbing down from his bunk. "What can I do?"

"Right now you can get ready to eat. After breakfast perhaps you—I should not ask—but perhaps you would be getting my deer for me."

David grinned. "You'll make me into a poacher yet!"

Heinie owned a toboggan, which he had left beside the slain deer. It was his means of transporting supplies to his cabin in winter, he explained. "Mr. Wilson many times makes the trip with horses," he said, "but when I am not lame, I like to walk down and go into town. Too much aloneness is not good for a man."

David struck out right after breakfast. The wind had swept bare many of the slopes and filled the hollows with snow, but he did not doubt his ability to backtrack his path of the night before. He would find the deer, Heinie said, a scant hundred yards below the spot where they had met.

As he strode along the trail, David did not devote too much thought to the rightness or wrongness of what he was doing. Heinie had broken the law, but to refuse to help the old man and let the meat spoil would benefit no one. The morning was sunny and pleasant, and he let his mind wander to other matters. Somehow it seemed as if he had been away from home much longer than just overnight. Johnny would be leaving for school about now, he supposed. Had the tall redhead and his cousin found Etonhill Princess Tanya?"

From a distance he saw the toboggan and the deer. Heinie had said that he flopped the dressed carcass face down on a snowbank to cool, but it appeared to be lying on its side. As David approached, a magpie rose chattering from the heap of entrails cast to one side. Immediately another of the handsome black-and-white scavengers flew up from the deer itself, and then he noticed the dog tracks. Had Tanya been drawn by the scent of fresh blood!

He studied the footprints in the snow. Unquestionably they had been made by the same dog that Link and Johnny had set out to track down the day before. From the looks of the deer, she had glutted herself. "Good for you, old gal," David applauded.

He scanned the draw for a sight of the German shepherd. "Tanya! Here, Tanya!" he called.

The magpies jeered at him from atop a boulder nearby, but the dog did not appear. "Probably filled her stomach, then holed up somewhere to sleep," David surmised aloud.

He called several times more, then on impulse uttered the shrill whistle with which he had always summoned Flash. Instantly he wished he hadn't. His throat tightened up and he nearly cried. Flash would have enjoyed every minute of last night's adventure and this morning's hike.

If Tanya heard, she did not respond. David followed her tracks to the point where they vanished on bare ground. Locating the valuable show dog might take some doing, he realized.

He returned to the deer and quickly loaded it on the toboggan, anchoring it securely with ropes. When he reached the cabin nearly an hour later, Heinie was watching for him. Together they hung the carcass from a horizontal pole lashed between two trees. Without a moment's delay, the old prospector fell to work with his skinning knife.

"Did Mr. Wilson call with any word for me?" David asked.

"The line is dead. Sometime in the night it is breaking. Don't worry, Davy, someone will come for you."

David had not thought to worry. He had just wondered. However, judging from Heinie's haste, he suspected that the old man was worried, worried that someone would see the poached deer.

The skinning was accomplished in minutes, and David helped to carry the carcass into the cabin. Heinie had not been idle. He had cleared away the breakfast dishes and laid out freezer paper and tape, assorted knives, a saw, and a large empty pasteboard carton.

The old man was an expert butcher. Within fifty minutes the bones, with every scrap of meat stripped from them, and a few gun-shot and magpie-spoiled scraps "for my friend the coyote" were in the box, and on the table were neat separate piles of steaks, chops, roasts, and stew meat.

"Maybe your friend the coyote will share with Tanya," David suggested. "You know, you might be able to lure her here by setting out food."

They wrapped the meat, labeled it, and put it in the freezing compartment of the refrigerator. "You take away the bones, and a deer is not very big," Heinie said. "Well, I very much thank you, Davy."

"I'm the one who should be doing the thanking," David replied. "If I hadn't run onto you last night, there's no telling where I might have ended up. I was lost and scared, and I was getting tired."

Heinie shrugged. "You could have stepped into the timber out of the wind and built a fire."

"Not this Boy Scout. I knew I'd be with Link, and he's so efficient I never thought to bring along anything to build a fire with."

"You will remember matches another time," Heinie assured him.

They heard the coyote sing as they prepared their noon meal. "Tonight, little wolf, you shall have a feast," the old man promised.

"Don't you get lonesome sometimes, Heinie? Wouldn't a dog be a lot of company?"

"Yah, I love dogs. But, Davy, I will die here one day, and who will be taking care of my dog? It is not fair that I own a dog."

"You shouldn't feel that way," David protested.

The little prospector shook his head. "Suppose I die one night? Maybe the telephone doesn't work. Nobody knows if I am here to answer. One day somebody comes and my dog have starved to death shut in the cabin."

"Well, that's not apt to happen. I'd think you'd want a dog."

"Do you have a dog, Davy?"

"I had one."

He told the old man about Flash. His throat muscles thickened, but his voice did not break. "If we had found Tanya, I was going to take my share of the reward money and start looking around for another sheltie. A good one costs a lot of money, and I want to get a good one."

"Well, I tell you, Davy. If I find this Princess Tanya, I will be splitting the reward, and you can buy this dog you want."

"No. No, the money would be yours."

They were arguing in friendly fashion when a shout outside the cabin brought them both to the window. "It is young Lincoln Ittlesby," said Heinie. "He has brought a horse for you to ride. Tell him we are almost to eat and ask him in.

David breathed a sigh of relief to see that the led horse was Shorty. He opened the door and relayed Heinie's invitation.

"You bet!" Link said. "I didn't bring any lunch. I was supposed to get up here and back by noon. But, David, I saw her tracks again! I followed them until they ran out on a bare hilltop. I looked all over, but I couldn't pick them up again."

"I saw her tracks this morning, too," David said. "I wish

Johnny and I could skip school tomorrow, but I know Dad would never let me."

"Saturday may be too late," Link warned as he came into the cabin. "Last night, before Mr. Wilson telephoned, we started calling the neighbors to see if you'd showed up anywhere. Pa was talking to Mr. Jutes, and when he told him we were hunting Tanya, Mr. Jutes said he'd shot at a German police dog that was prowling around his sheep."

"Oh, no!" David interjected.

"He missed her, but somebody else may get her without knowing how valuable she is."

"Hey! That reminds me," Link interrupted himself. "Price Sargent called Pa this morning after talking to Mr. Eton—Tanya's owner, you know? He says . . ." Link stopped abruptly. "Have you told Heinie?"

David nodded.

"Well, all right then. Mr. Eton told Price Sargent to offer a thousand-dollar reward. That's if Tanya is found and returned in good shape. They just bred her, and she's supposed to have puppies in November."

"For one thousand dollars," said Heinie, "I am thinking your pa might look for this dog."

"He's going to tomorrow. Our schoolhouse is fixed, but I'm going to see if he'll let me stay out one more day."

If Link recognized his steak as venison, he showed no concern. Perhaps he thought the meat came from the freezer and was last year's legal game. He ate with enthusiasm and made no comment. David decided privately that he would never tell what he knew.

When the boys prepared to depart, Heinie begged David to promise that he would come again. "If an excuse is needed," the old prospector said, "bring me batteries for my radio. Since August it is not working."

The ride down to the ranch house developed no interesting side lights. When David complained of aching knees, Link lengthened the stirrups a notch, and David discovered that the minor adjustment made an astounding difference. Given time, he believed he might learn to enjoy horseback riding.

Mrs. Ittlesby took him into town and let him off in front of his home just at dark. Incredibly, as he strode up the walk, he was hungry again. When he opened the front door he inhaled appreciatively the good smells of frying chicken and hot bread. Dad was sitting in his recliner rocker reading the evening paper; Harvey was lying on the floor.

Harvey was the first to look up. "Hey, Mom, David's home! David, look!"

He saw then that his brother was playing with a puppy. At a glance its pushed-in face and short, nicely marked coat suggested a Boston terrier, but its floppy ears looked distinctly spaniel-ish. "Yeah, cute pup," David said. "Whose is it?"

"Mine."

"Yours!"

Marshall Hollis laid aside his paper just as Mom hurried into the front room. "Well, hello, son," he said.

"Hi, honey!" Mom exclaimed. Taking him by the arms, she gave him a big welcoming squeeze. "Come get your coat off and wash up for supper. I want to hear all about your adventures."

David grinned at her and returned the affectionate

squeeze. "Hi, Mom. Hi, Dad. Hey, what's the scoop on the pup?"

"He's mine, I told you," Harvey said.

David ignored the younger boy. "That's right," Dad confirmed. "The pup belongs to Harvey."

"But, Dad, that's a mutt! I mean, why didn't you get him a purebred? Harve doesn't need a show dog, but, gee whiz, he won't even be able to enter this pup in obedience trials."

"No, and thank goodness!" said the elder Hollis.

"But, Dad . . ."

His father sighed. "Look, son. You had the last dog. This is Harvey's dog. Harvey doesn't need a purebred."

"But . . . but I sort of planned on getting another sheltie."

"David, we don't need a sheltie. We have a dog. One dog in the family is enough. I think it's time you quit wasting all of your time and most of your money on dogs."

"Aw, Dad, I . . ."

"Let's drop it," Marshall Hollis suggested brusquely. "The subject is closed!"

4.

Heinie's Secret

The disappearance of Champion Etonhill Princess Tanya
became the local news event of the year. The people of
Winnegar, content with their small-town ways, had
laughed when one of the community's wealthier citizens
had paid three hundred and fifty dollars for a bird dog.
They could scarcely conceive of a dog worth one thousand dollars.

On the first weekend following the plane crash, the
Ittlesby ranch boasted more dog hunters per square mile
than cattle. The search for Tanya became the favorite
avocation of the whole county—men, women, and children. The weather cooperated—or didn't cooperate—
according to the viewpoint of the individual. Pleasant
Indian summer days saw the searchers hiking in their
shirt sleeves, but there was no snow for tracking.

So often was Tanya sighted that the astute reader of the
daily newspaper soon concluded that the German shepherd dog was quintuplets. She raided a chicken house
fifteen miles north of town and within the hour was seen
chasing a colt in a pasture twelve miles south of town.

David and Johnny and Link joined the treasure-seeking
horde the first weekend. Assuming that Tanya would
linger in the vicinity of the crashed plane, the boys felt
their chances of finding her were better than average because Link knew the country. However, they neither saw
her nor talked to anyone else who saw her.

"I'll bet Mr. Jutes hit her when he shot at her, and she's crawled off somewhere to die," Link asserted with conviction.

Within two weeks the reward offered for the safe return of the dog had swelled to over fourteen hundred dollars. German shepherd dog specialty clubs across the nation were voting donations to the fund. Not only was Tanya herself of prime importance to the breed, but she had been bred to an international champion whose bloodlines complemented her own. Buyers waited in line to claim the puppies at five hundred a throw.

David talked to Heinie on the subject early in October, three weeks to the day after the plane crash. He had bought batteries for the old man's transistor radio, then hitched a ride to the Wilson ranch and hiked the two miles up the mountain to the old prospector's cabin.

"If the dog is not soon found," Heinie said, "I am thinking her puppies will be no good."

"Why?" David wanted to know.

"Because she is not a wild animal. She has since a puppy been finding her food in a dish. She will be always hungry, and the puppies inside her will not grow."

David nodded, but at the same time he had to smile. "I think every rancher in the county is putting out food, hoping to lure her into his hands."

"Yah, but is she finding this food? She is a tame dog. Why does she not go into some yard and say, 'I am here. Feed me'?"

Heinie pointed his finger at David. "I'll tell you why, Davy. Mr. Wesley Jutes shot at her and she is afraid. She is either dead, or she is on purpose staying away from people."

"You're probably right," David admitted. "The paper keeps printing reports of people who have sighted her, but who knows what they're really seeing?"

"I tell you what we'll do, Davy. When it comes Christmas and you have a vacation, there will be snow. You come up and stay with ol' Heinie a few days, and we will look around, yah?"

"It's a deal!" David told him.

When the time came for David to leave, the old man insisted on walking part way down the trail with him. "I still wear the bandage, but my ankle is not hurting any more. You must come soon again, Davy."

David did mean to go back and visit the old man, but time got away from him. He made the basketball B squad, and basketball became almost a way of life. When no games were scheduled, there was drill or a practice game. A time or two he went with Johnny to dog obedience classes. Then on a Saturday morning near the end of November, David received a phone call from Mrs. Wilson. "Heinie wants to know if you have forgotten him. He asked me to find out whether you would be coming to see him some day soon."

David spun his mental wheels. He had to play that night, and he was supposed to get some jobs done around home this weekend. Next Friday and Saturday was the Christmas invitational basketball tournament. He wouldn't play, but there would be a lot going on. Sunday he and Johnny planned to watch the snowmobile races. The whole week after that was crowded with Christmas activities. He hadn't even begun to think about shopping yet.

"I'd better come see him tomorrow," he decided aloud.

If he delayed, he would not get away until the week between Christmas and New Year's.

He thanked Mrs. Wilson for calling and hung up. Now,
he thought, to persuade Mom to take him to the Wilson
ranch. He knew a couple of guys with cars, but he didn't
want to include either of them in his and Heinie's plans.
Mom was a good bet because she could drop him off at
the Wilson ranch and drive on up the valley to see a
cousin who owned a farm.

On the surface the idea looked great, but it backfired.
Mom agreed immediately to serve as taxi driver. "But,"
she said, "I wasn't planning to visit Edna this early. I
haven't my Christmas candies made. I'll take you out to
the Wilsons' tomorrow on one condition. As soon as the
ball game is over tonight, you come straight home and
help me make candy."

"That's blackmail!" David yelped.

"That's seizing opportunity when it knocks," Cleo Hollis
replied tartly.

At one-thirty the next afternoon she let him off in the
Wilson dooryard. The snow was beaten down around the
buildings and corrals, but on the hill it came almost to the
tops of his four-buckle overshoes. Mrs. Wilson had asked
him to carry a back pack of supplies for Heinie, and the
heavy going soon had him sweating. When finally he
topped the long uphill grade and could look across to the
ravine where bootleggers had once concocted their illegal
brew, he paused to catch his breath. A thin streamer of
smoke rising from the timber pinpointed the location of
the cabin.

He stood breathing deeply, a quiet feeling of satisfaction welling in him. He could understand Heinie's love of

the mountains. Up here was solitude but not necessarily loneliness.

Very soon the cold air began to penetrate his exposed shirt front, and he moved on across the sage-dotted bench. Where the trail forked at the mouth of the ravine, he was startled by the sudden clamorous barking of a dog. He stiffened in surprise. He knew at a glance the German shepherd that bounded toward him through the snow. No common dog this, with coarse head and lopsided gait. This animal, despite a certain raggedness of coat and sagging, milk-filled nipples, possessed symmetry and grace and that indefinable quality that is simply class.

"Tanya!"

David spoke sharply and laughed to see her stop in midstride, astonished that a stranger should call her name.

"Hi, Tanya!"

The dog growled softly and held her distance, but at the same time her tail swung in a slow arc. A life in the show ring had taught Etonhill Princess Tanya tolerance toward all people. Her natural instinct to guard and protect had been deliberately and systematically suppressed.

Up the ravine the cabin door slammed, and David glanced up to see Heinie striding his way.

"Princess, Princess, you don't bite our Davy! Hallo, Davy! What do you think of my dog? Pretty fine dog, yah?"

Gaily Tanya trotted to the old man's side and nuzzled his hand. She barked again at David, but her long tail moved in a full sweep. She understood tone and inflection if not the actual words.

David moved forward. "She has puppies, hasn't she? Are they all right? Where did you find her, Heinie?"

"Come," said the old man.

Tanya galloped ahead and stood on her hind legs to scratch and pound at the cabin's door. When Heinie opened it, she dashed across the small room and hopped into a low-sided pen constructed of rough, weathered boards. Instantly a chorus of eager puppy voices erupted. She nosed the babies as if swiftly counting, then looked up and wagged her tail, her dark eyes glistening with pride.

David followed Heinie around the table. "How many are there?"

"Seven. Or perhaps only six and two-thirds. One little girl is much smaller."

Together they squatted by the makeshift whelping box. The seven puppies sprawling on a tattered blanket looked nearly identical. They were black with tan markings that were just beginning to show well. All were chubby and vigorous, even the runt.

"How old are they, Heinie?"

"Two weeks. Two days ago their eyes are opening."

Tanya lay down and the squirming youngsters, not yet able to walk, crowded and pushed as they sought her milk. The runt found a nipple but was thrust aside by a bigger puppy. She grabbed another nipple and a second time was jostled away. Tumbled to the edge of the heap, she rolled out on the blanket all by herself and began to wail.

"Ah, little one, do not despair. Ol' Heinie will help you."

Gently the old man picked up the littlest puppy and held her so that she too could drink. Soon all whimperings ceased and the only sounds from the seven puppies were tiny sucking noises and the smacking of baby lips.

David watched entranced as the puppies quickly filled their stomachs. Some of them fell asleep still clinging to their dam. "What's the story, Heinie?"

"Put down your burden, Davy. Take off your jacket. Here, you must sit down."

In his excitement over the puppies, David had forgotten the rucksack he carried. "Don't know what this stuff is," he said. "Mrs. Wilson said you asked her to send it up."

He dropped the pack onto a chair. "Where do you want me to put it?"

"First, look and see what you have," advised Heinie.

His curiosity aroused, David unfastened the straps and lifted the canvas flap. "Powdered milk—two big boxes of powdered milk—a bag of oatmeal, cod-liver oil, powdered egg yolks, and . . . what's in this brown bottle?"

He pulled out the quart bottle and saw it bore a druggist's label. "Lime water," he read.

"To make strong bones," Heinie explained. "You see sometimes puppies with badly crooked legs. Rickets is caused by not enough Vitamin D and not enough calcium. So the cod-liver oil, and we put a little lime water in the milk. We give it to our Princess now, and in another week to the puppies, when they begin to eat and drink from a dish."

David regarded the old man in amazement. "I didn't know you knew so much about dogs."

Heinie smiled. "One time in the Park I am finding a litter of baby coyotes only a few days old. Something has happened to their papa and mama and they are starving. So I got a book, and they grew up fine and strong."

"Gee, Tanya is sure lucky you found her instead of somebody else. Hey, tell me about it!"

The little prospector shrugged. "Some hunter shot her, I think. It must have been somebody who does not live here and did not know of the reward. I followed a bloody trail to her den. She has been living not a mile from here. When I bring her to the cabin, she have the puppies that night."

"She doesn't seem to be lame or anything now," David observed.

Heinie leaned to stroke the dog. Although Tanya lay quietly, her dark eyes followed the old man's every move. "The bullet grazed her foreleg. See? It is almost healed."

David asked many questions. The last and perhaps the most important was, "When I go back to town today, do you want me to call Etonhill Kennels?"

Heinie considered. "If you call that Mr. Sargent, he will come and take our Princess and her puppies. They are too young to be traveling."

"Oh, I'd tell him that," David assured the old man.

"No, I think we should wait. Maybe the puppies, some of them, do not survive. I think later is soon enough."

"They're doing fine," David argued. "Even the runt. She isn't as fat as the others, but she's wiry and strong."

"Ah, Davy, let an old man play with his toys! Soon enough they will have to go."

David grinned. "So that's it! Okay, I'll hold off awhile."

"You won't tell anyone?"

"Not if you don't want me to," David promised. "What about Mrs. Wilson, though? Won't she suspect from all this stuff you ordered?"

The old man smiled. "I told her I am finding a coyote pup."

Too soon David had to leave. His mother would be

waiting. As he bent to give Tanya a farewell pat, he said,
"I agree with Heinie, girl. They should have called you
Princess. You really are a royal princess!"

"You come back in two or three weeks," Heinie urged.
"The puppies will be old enough then to stand a trip."

David didn't see that he could possibly get back before
Christmas; yet he knew he would find the time. The seven
furry babies would draw him as a magnet draws iron.

Somehow he got through the activities of the next three
weeks—basketball, special programs at church and in
school, Johnny's dog class graduation, and six-weeks'
exams. On Friday, the twentieth, school let out for Christmas, and on Saturday afternoon David hitched a ride to
the Wilson ranch. Despite blue skies and a brilliant sun,
the day was crisply cold. He whistled as he started up the
trail with a box containing two apple pies Mom had baked
especially for Heinie.

As on the occasion of his last visit, his presence was
noted and announced almost from the instant he set foot
on the trail leading into Bootleggers' Ravine. Tanya recognized him this time, however, and came to him when he
called. He thumped her ribs, and was pleased to find her
in good flesh.

Heinie stood waiting at the cabin door. "Hallo, Davy! I
knew you would come. Come in!"

At once he saw that another round of boards had been
added to the sides of the puppy pen. Even so, big baby
paws reached to the top and bright, dark eyes peered over
the barrier.

"Gee, they've grown!"

The litter looked terrific. At a glance David could not
even identify the runt. He presented the pies to Heinie,

then knelt to pick up a pudgy, wriggling puppy, being very careful to lift it by the body rather than by the front legs. A professional handler had once warned him that a puppy's shoulders could be permanently injured by careless early handling.

"Hi, fella! Hi, little hot-shot!"

He stood up, trying without much success to cuddle the active baby. It showed promise of beautiful markings. The tan color was stealing up its legs and highlighting the neck and flanks. David looked to see if the other puppies were as attractive and suddenly he realized that there remained only five in the pen.

"Hey, the runt's gone!" he exclaimed. That was why the litter had seemed so uniform!

Heinie nodded. "Mr. Eton of Etonhill will be glad to get the six."

"Oh, he'll be tickled sick. But, gee, it's too bad about the runt. Boy, Heinie, you don't know how hard it's been not to tell anyone about these pups. I'll bet Price Sargent will just go wild when he hears the news."

"Yah, I am thinking he will be pleased," the old man agreed. "Today, Davy, when you go, you will take the toboggan and the puppies, and Princess will go with you. You will call Etonhill today, yah?"

"Okay," David replied. "And should I have them send me the reward money so I can bring it to you?"

"Whatever you wish. We are partners, Davy. You must go soon now, so if you are having any trouble it does not get too late." He sounded almost eager to be rid of his charges, as if, having resigned himself to the inevitable, he could not bear to prolong the parting.

The old man had fashioned a long narrow crate to fit

the toboggan. They placed the puppies in the box and wired the slatted top securely in place. "We'll drape this blanket over them," said Heinie. "There will still be air to breathe, but they will stay warm."

Tanya cocked her head as whimpers of protest began to issue from under the blanket. She whined her concern and scratched at the crate. "You're going to miss these little fellers, Heinie," David said.

"I will miss them, yah." The old man shrugged. "But lately they are much work. You must go now, Davy."

Tanya scarcely knew what to do. As David started down the trail with the toboggan, she trotted alongside for a few steps, then ran back to Heinie. "I don't want you!" the old man said sharply. "Go on. Go with Davy!"

She looked at him, taken aback by the harshness in his voice. Her tail drooped. Just then the toboggan jolted against a rock under the snow and a puppy yelped in fear as he was jostled by his fellows. In that instant Tanya made her decision. She raced to catch up with the crate.

David encountered no difficulty on the hike down to the Wilson ranch. Time and again Tanya would stop and look back over her shoulder, but she did not intend to abandon her puppies. When David strode into the barnyard with the toboggan and its freight, only Mr. Wilson was home. The rancher was astounded to see Tanya. "Sure hope the wife and kids get home in time to see the puppies," he said.

David hoped they wouldn't. Tanya's offspring weren't the kind you turn over to just anybody to handle.

As if on cue, Cleo Hollis arrived. "I'm sorry to rush you," she called as she braked to a stop, "but your father needs the car. That's a lovely dog you have, Mr. Wilson."

The rancher blinked. "Oh, that's not my dog, missus. She's that show champion that got lost. David just brought her and the pups down from the hills."

"He what!"

David walked over grinning. "Hand me the trunk key, Mom. Got to load this crate."

Before his mother could make up her mind to protest, he had the trunk open, and Mr. Wilson bent to help him lift the crate. Tanya put her front feet up on the bumper in order to supervise. The puppies were loaded and David spread the blanket again.

"Let me get you a baling string to tie that trunk lid and keep it from flying up," offered Mr. Wilson.

"David, what is this all about?" Mom demanded.

For answer he opened the door into the back seat of the car. "Come on, Tanya!"

With a single bound the German shepherd mounted the seat. Pink tongue lolling and tail wagging, she poked her long wolf muzzle into the face of a surprised Cleo Hollis.

"Mom, meet Ch. Etonhill Princess Tanya!"

He remembered, while Mr. Wilson secured the trunk lid, to ask what he should do with Heinie's toboggan. When everything had been taken care of, he climbed in beside his mother. "Drive carefully," he cautioned. "We've got valuable cargo."

On the way home he told the whole story. "I'll call Price Sargent right away," he concluded. "I'll bet he flies into Bozeman tomorrow morning."

Marshall Hollis flew out of the house the minute they arrived. A minor emergency had arisen and he had been waiting for the car. "Good night!" he exclaimed when he was made aware of the vehicle's canine occupants. "What if that California outfit refuses to claim them!"

"Don't worry," David assured him. "They'll come running as soon as I call them."

With window screens and the dubious help of Harvey's pup Muggins, he constructed a temporary pen for the puppies in the basement. Tanya fed her offspring, then followed him upstairs. As he sat at the phone waiting for his long-distance call to get through to the Etonhill Kennels, the thought occurred to him that Price Sargent might be in another city attending a dog show. However, a kennel boy answered and promptly summoned the famous handler.

David identified himself and mentioned that he lived in Winnegar, Montana. "I've called to tell you that I have Princess Tanya," he announced, his palms wet with perspiration born of excitement.

"That so?" came the bored reply. "What makes you think so?"

Stunned by the man's indifference, David heard himself stammering. "Why . . . because . . . why, it's Tanya, that's all. There . . ."

"Have you checked with your local authorities? Your sheriff's office there has had at least a dozen 'Tanyas' brought in since September twenty-sixth. I don't mean to disappoint you, kid, but the chances of that dog being alive now are one in a thousand."

"But, Mr. Sargent," David protested, "there aren't any other German shepherds around here of anything like Tanya's quality."

"What's that, son?" said Sargent, his voice sharpening

with interest. "You just said something. You said 'quality.' Do you know anything about German shepherds?"

"Not a whole lot, sir," David confessed, "but I go to dog shows and obedience trials. I've seen quite a few German shepherds. There's no mistake about Tanya, sir. She had a den about half a mile from where your plane crashed."

"What shape is she in?"

"Oh, she's in real good condition. Heinie Wehring—he's an old man, a . . . a prospector—he found her just before the puppies were born. She's fine, and the puppies look really . . ."

"Oh, great!" exploded Sargent. "Why weren't we notified five weeks ago? Those pups at birth were worth five hundred bucks apiece!"

"Well, they . . . the puppies are fine," David insisted timidly.

"I'll bet! Scrawny, wormy, pot-gutted, and probably rickety! Why weren't we contacted?"

"Because . . ." David started to explain, then found his own temper flaring. "They are not rickety!" he snapped. "Heinie put lime water in their milk, and he fed them codliver oil and eggs and meat, and they're big and fat and real shiny and healthy. And Tanya's not scrawny either!"

For a moment silence filled the line. David heard the man on the other end release a long sigh. Then Price Sargent spoke in a much subdued tone. "I'm sorry, kid. I could just picture the whole litter ruined by some well-meaning but ignorant farm hand. You say Tanya is in good shape and the puppies have had care by someone who knows something about dogs?"

From that moment David had no further trouble communicating with the famous dog handler. He told all that he knew about Tanya and her puppies and answered what questions he could.

"Look, kid," Sargent said finally. "Here's what I want you to do. Check with the sheriff there and get a positive identification. I don't see how it could be any other dog, but we won't take chances. Then call the airport that's nearest you and see what arrangements can be made to ship the dogs here. Order a separate crate for the pups. You'll get the reward for Tanya, of course, and if the litter is in the shape you say it is, there'll be a bonus."

He had David write down a long list of specific directions. The dogs must be checked by a veterinarian before shipment. Insurance must be secured. "Be sure to let me know when to meet the plane on this end. And listen, kid . . . what's your name again?"

David told him.

"Okay, David. Keep track of all your expenses and get a list of the old man's expenses. We'll make it right with you."

The next couple of days were the most exciting of David's life. He followed to the letter the instructions given him by Price Sargent. He put Tanya and her family on a plane the next morning. His father provided transportation to and from the airport at Bozeman, Montana. Dogs were not foolishness when fifteen-hundred dollars' reward money hung in the balance. David became a celebrity overnight as Winnegar's only daily paper devoted a full page to pictures of him and the dogs and ran a front-page story on Heinie Wehring's recovery of the valuable animals.

Tuesday's mail brought a personal note from millionaire Walter Eton and a check from Etonhill Kennels in the amount of seventeen hundred dollars. Tanya and her puppies had arrived in excellent condition. Eton was delighted to pay the bonus as promised by his kennel manager, and as soon as David could present a bill for his expenses, he would see that it was given prompt attention.

That afternoon David persuaded his mother to take him once more to the Wilson ranch. "It's really Heinie's money, Mom, and tomorrow is Christmas. I've got to let him know today."

He felt like singing as he hiked up the familiar trail. A brisk wind swirling the snow reminded him of his first meeting with the little prospector. It had been a fortuitous meeting. "He'll be tickled about the money, but I'll bet he's really missing those pups about now," David told himself.

Heinie evidently saw him coming, for the door swung wide as David mounted the big flat stone that served as a doorstep. "Davy! Come in! Welcome!"

"Merry Christmas, Hei— . . . WHAT'S THAT?" David broke off in midsentence.

Behind the old man, in the middle of the floor, stood a small, plump, bright-eyed German shepherd puppy.

5.

David Makes a Promise

"That?" Heinie repeated, turning to look at the German shepherd puppy. "That is Blitz."

Stiffly the old man got down on one knee. "Blitz, come see our friend Davy."

Tail jaunty, the puppy pranced forward. Her baby confidence would have melted the coldest heart.

"But, Heinie, that's one of Tanya's pups! That's the runt. I thought you said she had died."

The little prospector took the puppy gently in his hands. "She was asleep on my bed the day you came to take the Princess. I hadn't planned to keep her, Davy, but you jumped to the conclusion that she was dead, and I thought . . ." Heinie shrugged. "I thought, let them think she is dead."

"But she belongs to Etonhill Kennels," David objected.

"No, Davy. Five weeks ago, if I don't feed this puppy by hand and hold her and warm her, she is dead. I stayed up with her four nights. She is mine."

David hardly knew what to say. He disagreed with his friend. He felt that Heinie was wrong, although he could sort of see the old man's viewpoint. Belatedly he remembered the certified check in his pocket.

"Heinie, they sent you seventeen hundred dollars. That's the reward with two hundred extra for taking such good care of the puppies."

The old man got to his feet, holding the puppy close. "We split it, eh, Davy?"

David shook his head. "You found Tanya and did all the work. Mr. Sargent told me to send him a bill for my expenses. That's all I want."

"No, we are partners, Davy!" Abruptly the old man smiled. "You helped me to poach a deer and the Princess ate it. This gave her milk for the puppies."

"But I didn't even help you look for—for Princess."

"Ah, Davy, take off your coat and we will sit down."

While they discussed the money, Heinie held the puppy and loved her with his hands and with his eyes. "She is a runt," he said defensively. "She is not of interest to Etonhill. They have six, and they are happy."

David could have argued with the old man, but he held his peace. Although Blitz might never enter a show ring, might never be good enough to show, she had the same flawless bloodlines as her brothers and sisters. She was valuable because of her potential as breeding stock.

"Send them back my share of the reward," Heinie growled, as if reading his thoughts. "Tell them I am keeping her."

"They would take her away from you," David said. "I don't think the money means anything at all to Mr. Eton, but if he let you keep this puppy, he'd always worry that she might turn out to be the best one."

"Then don't tell him. You keep the money. Keep it all. I am keeping Blitz."

David shrugged. What Heinie decided to do with the puppy was *his* business, he guessed. "Where did you get that name for her, Heinie?"

"Blitz? Blitz is German for lightning. She is learning anything like lightning. It is a good name, yah?"

"Yeah," David agreed. "I never thought about it before, but you know that Christmas poem? 'Up Dancer, up Prancer, on Donner and Blitzen.' That's Thunder and Lightning, isn't it?"

"Blitzen is wrong. It is Blitz."

David grinned and reached to fondle the puppy's furry head. "Well, little Blitz, you're a pretty cute kid."

"I will tell people I bought her. She is a runt. Nobody will care."

They talked only a few minutes longer. David finally agreed to accept two hundred dollars of the reward money, provided he had his friend's permission to split a hundred of that between Johnny and Link. "I'd never have met you, Heinie, if it hadn't been for those guys," he explained.

He had to leave then. His mother had driven on up to see her cousin but did not expect to stay. The day before Christmas was no time to tie up the activities of busy people. When he reached the Wilson ranch yard, she sat waiting, motor running.

"How is Heinie? Lonesome?" she asked.

"Oh, he's fine," David replied. All the way down the mountain he had wrestled with his conscience, and he had finally concluded that he had no right to set himself up as judge.

"He's fine," he repeated. "He insists on giving me part of the reward money. Do you think there's any chance Dad will let me buy another sheltie?"

Mom tossed him a sidelong glance. "David, I think you

know it's not the money. Your father feels you spend too much of your time and energy on dogs. You'll soon be sixteen, and you should be thinking about college and a career."

"Maybe I'm thinking of becoming a professional dog handler like Price Sargent," David retorted. He wasn't. He hadn't until that moment ever considered the possibility.

"Well, I wouldn't mention it to your father, if I were you," Cleo Hollis said wearily.

"Well, gee whiz, Mom, wouldn't you rather I was spending my money on dogs and going to dog shows than buying beer and running around with a bunch of guys in a souped-up jalopy?"

His mother sighed. "Your father isn't convinced that either dogs or carousing is necessary. However, I will talk to him, David. I'll try to get him to see your point of view."

Traditionally the Hollis family opened their gifts on Christmas morning. The only present David really wanted was a Sheltie, or, if not the dog in the flesh, at least permission to buy one. He got neither, and the pile of loot he received did little to satisfy his emptiness of spirit.

Shortly before noon Johnny called. His dad had bought their family a pair of two-man snowmobiles and a trailer with which to transport them—the works. Would David like to go with the Martzes that afternoon and help break in the new equipment?

David would and did, and Christmas was salvaged.

The first semester of the school year ended in mid-January. When David made the honor roll, he signed up to take driver training the next six weeks and won from his father a promise that he could buy a car if he main-

tained a B average to the end of the school year. Johnny
Martz turned sixteen in February. He passed the tests for
his driver's license, and the very next Saturday afternoon
he loaded a snowmobile on the trailer and picked up
David to go see Heinie. David had not been back to the
cabin since the day before Christmas. He had told Johnny
about Blitz and sworn him to secrecy. His friend was as
anxious to see the puppy as he was.

As they started out from the Wilson yard Shad galloped
alongside. Nobody enjoyed the snowmobiles more than
the big collie. David did not envy Johnny his driving priv-
ileges or his use of the family sports equipment, but he
did envy him his dog.

From the top of the hill they could see chimney smoke
curling up out of the timber. When they reached the cabin, however, and cut the engine, Heinie did not appear.
Then, before David could dismount to knock, they heard
a power saw whine into action on up the ravine.

"Bet he's getting firewood," Johnny deduced. "Hang
on!"

Following the track of the toboggan, they came upon
the old man a couple of hundred yards above the cabin.
Blitz was with him, a gangling weed of a dog, all feet and
awkwardness. One ear stood erect, the other flopped. She
barked a warning, then ran to sit on Heinie's feet as Shad
trotted toward her to investigate.

The little prospector apparently did not see that David
was seated behind Johnny. He picked up a stick with
which to warn Shad away and peered at Johnny, obviously puzzled as to the identity of his visitor. David
jumped off almost before the snow machine came to a
halt. "Hi, Heinie," he called. "We came to see Blitz."

"Oh, it is Davy! Blitz, it is Davy!"

The old man was taking advantage of a pleasant day to cut fallen trees into stove lengths. "I am not short yet," he said, "but I burn more fuel this winter. I seem to get always cold."

He had piled part of a load on the toboggan and was cutting more. "I work so slowly," he said in apology. "This power saw is worth twenty men with axes, but it is a heavy booger. I rest more than I work."

The boys exchanged glances and because they were friends reached agreement without words. "Let me use the saw awhile," David offered. "You and Johnny can load up the toboggan and pull it down to the cabin behind the snowmobile."

Heinie started to protest, but Johnny firmly overruled him. "David and I need the exercise."

"Well, that is okay. But I better show you how to run this thing."

Two hours later, the three of them sat at Heinie's table and drank hot chocolate. Blitz lay down beside the slightly built old man who was her master and utterly ignored the boys. She wasn't shy. She simply had no time for anyone but Heinie.

"She sure has grown," David remarked, stroking the indifferent puppy.

"Yah, I think she is not a runt any more."

"How come she has a flop ear? What happened to it?" Johnny asked.

"Nothing happened. It will stand up when the muscles in the ear grow stronger. The other one just came up. This one stands up sometimes."

As they talked, David looked at Heinie with increasing

concern. The old man looked positively frail. He had lost weight. His hollow cheeks were pasty, his bony hands almost transparent. It seemed to David that in a few weeks he had aged years.

"Are you feeling all right, Heinie?" he asked finally.

"Yah. Today, pretty good."

"Have you been sick?"

The old man shrugged. "I am not well for a long time."

"Have you been to a doctor?"

"Doctors only want to put you in the hospital. I am not wishing to go to the hospital."

"But, gee, if you've got something wrong . . ."

"Sometimes, Davy, you cannot fix a worn-out machine. You just run it until it quits."

The boys exchanged shocked glances. In the uncomfortable silence Heinie continued. "I made a mistake, Davy. I should not have kept Blitz. I cannot give her up now, but I should not have kept her. Someday you will have to take care of her for me. Will you promise me you will do that, Davy?"

"Sure, I'll take care of her, but you're not going anywhere. You'll be around for a long time, Heinie."

"Yah. Yah, I talk too much. You must forgive an old man."

The subject was quickly changed, but the uneasiness remained. The boys did not stay long. Johnny had promised to be home by dark. Although nothing more was said about Heinie's health, the memory of the old man's sunken cheeks was to haunt David for weeks to come. Somehow he had come to feel responsible for the little prospector. He worried about his living alone, worried that the ancient telephone line might be broken at some crucial time.

Yet he did not see Heinie again until May. He had run into a supermarket during his school lunch hour, and he stopped short at sight of a shabby little man loading canned goods into a shopping cart. The old fellow had his back turned, but he surely looked like Heinie.

Even as David hesitated, the shopper faced around and caught sight of him. "Davy! I am just wishing to see you!"

They had only a few minutes to visit. Mrs. Wilson was waiting in the parking lot to take Heinie home, and David had to get back to school. The meeting meant much to David, however. Heinie looked to be in better health than he had looked in February, and he said he felt better. Blitz, he declared, had become more beautiful than her mother. He had tied her up and left her at the Wilson ranch while he came to town, but David must come to see her.

"I have looked for you, Davy," the old man said.

David promised that he would try to get up for a visit soon, but time slipped away from him. School ended. He bought a much-used Chevy and the next day went to work building fence for Tom Ittlesby. His mother had hoped he might find something in town, but Marshall Hollis saw no objection to a ranch job. "Good hard work will build his muscles. I'd like to see him go out for football next year."

For the most part David liked his job. However, he worked five and a half days a week, and he didn't get to a single dog show on the Montana Copper Circuit, didn't get to see Johnny and Shad flunk Open A obedience four times straight.

On July second Mom phoned to report that Mrs. Wilson had called. She was concerned about Heinie. The telephone line to the cabin had been dead for several days, and she wondered if the Hollises had been keeping in touch. David decided right then to skip Winnegar's annual Fourth of July rodeo and make a trip too long postponed.

Right after breakfast on the morning of the Fourth he saddled Shorty. He considered driving to the Wilson ranch and hiking the two miles up to the cabin, but after a month of riding with Link he had developed a cowboy's disdain for foot travel. Shorty, he had been surprised to discover, was a good mount when you knew how to get the best out of him.

By midmorning the sun was broiling. Not a breath of wind stirred. Shorty swished his tail and bobbed his head constantly as nose flies and big stinging deer flies attacked without mercy. Cattle stood motionless in the timber. David dismounted to drink at nearly every creek he crossed and measured his progress from one watering place to the next.

The tiny clearing in front of Heinie's cabin seemed almost like an oven. The big trees offered no protection from a sun that beat down from directly overhead. When David reined up Blitz raised a fuss in the cabin, but Heinie did not put in an appearance. "Man, if I've missed him . . ." David muttered. He did not finish the thought.

He sat for a moment undecided. Where would Heinie have gone that he left Blitz behind?

Of his own accord Shorty turned toward the little creek whose tireless waters over the centuries had carved Bootleggers' Ravine. David dismounted and dropped the reins.

The day he met Heinie in the supermarket the old man had said that he left his dog tied in the Wilsons' yard. Surely, if he were prospecting or doing anything in the woods he would have taken her with him.

Despite the heat David felt a sudden chill. Was Heinie inside with Blitz?

He hesitated. The door probably was not locked, but he would hate to risk letting Blitz out if she were supposed to be shut in. Better to look in through a window.

Weeds grew waist-high against the cabin. He trampled them aside and bent to peer through a sagging screen. Instantly Blitz sounded off again. He cupped his hands around his eyes to cut the sun's glare and presently made out the shape of her in the dimness of the cabin's interior. The young shepherd stood backed against the bunk beds, her head held low, her ruff and the hair along her back stiffly erect.

A movement behind the dog drew David's eye. As he spied the slight, twisted form in the bottom bunk, an exclamation of dismay burst unbidden from his throat. In two strides he reached the cabin door. The latch yielded to his hand. Hinges creaked. A blast of hot, stale air enveloped him, and suddenly a snarling, raging Blitz was barring his path.

For a moment the young dog's ferocity jarred him. Instinctively he backed away. If German shepherd dogs as a breed had one fault, it lay, he knew, in their zeal to protect the human beings they loved. Their vice was not viciousness but overprotectiveness. Yet David was surprised to find the trait full-blown in an eight-month-old puppy.

"Take it easy, Blitz. Don't you know your old buddy, David?"

She pricked her ears at the sound of her own name but did not cease her racket. Heinie lay as though dead. "You've got to let me in, Blitz," David said.

She obviously had no such intention. He wasted several minutes trying to talk to her and finally picked up a stout stick. Filled with a sense of daring, he made as though to step boldly across the sill. When she lunged at him, he whacked not the dog but the doorjamb. He swung with such force that he broke his stick. She shied from the motion and flinched at the noise, and he took advantage of her momentary insecurity to slip into the room.

"Blitz, down!"

He gave the command as he moved toward the sink at the far end of the cabin. He didn't expect her to obey, and she didn't, but his tone of authority impressed her nevertheless. She fell silent and padded to the bunk where her master lay. Worriedly, she sought the old man's face with her long muzzle.

David wilted into a chair at the table. He had no idea how long Heinie had lain unconscious. The temperature in the room was surely a hundred and ten degrees. Blitz crouched by the bed, watching him, panting and growling by turn. He talked to her, and as he talked inspiration was born of the suffocating heat. There was no water dish on the floor. Apparently Heinie had relied on Blitz getting what water she needed from the creek. If she had been shut in very long, she must be desperately thirsty.

"How about a drink, old kid?" he asked conversationally.

She barked as he stood up and moved to the sink, but she made no move to attack. He pumped until the water flowed freely, deliberately letting it splash and gurgle.

"Sure you can have a drink," he cooed, "I'll just rinse out the wash basin and fill it. Come on, Blitz."

She followed him to the door and watched as he set the pan on the ground just out from the big flat rock. She whined and ran her tongue over dry lips. David did not try to coax her. Instead, he gambled and stepped toward the cabin. Blitz growled but retreated to let him in.

"It's out there, girl," he said softly. "Help yourself."

He sat again at the table, but closer to the door this time. Sweating, fighting a sense of urgency, he waited. Blitz paced restlessly, tempted by the water but plainly distrustful.

"You know me, Blitz, you big sap!"

In the lower bunk Heinie stirred. Blitz went to him instantly. David called the old man's name, but Heinie made no response. He lay on his back with his face turned toward the wall, his slow, irregular breathing plainly audible now that Blitz had quieted.

After a time the dog turned away and wandered across to the door. Her nostrils twitched at the smell of water. She glanced at David, who pretended not to notice, and uttered a little whine of indecision. Several times she circled, and finally she slipped out the door.

David moved so quickly that he knocked his chair over. Before the startled dog could divine his purpose he slammed the door shut behind her and secured it. He heard her squall of outrage and an instant later her body struck the heavy panel. He winced. He would not like to be within reach of her powerful young jaws.

Striding to the bunk, he bent over the still figure of the old man. "Heinie, Heinie, wake up!" he pleaded. He was almost afraid to touch his old friend.

Heinie gave no indication of hearing. David watched the slow rise and fall of the frail chest and tried to think. The heat in the cabin was enough to make a well person faint.

"Got to cool him off somehow."

He strode to the sink, found a washcloth, and wet it. Dripping a trail across the floor, he returned to the bunk and clumsily patted the old man's forehead. He held his breath to see the pale eyelids fluter and colorless lips move. He bent low to catch a whispered plea. "Water!"

Leaving the wet cloth, he ran to the pump. With hands made awkward by his haste, he filled the cup that always hung above the sink. "Here you go," he said, hurrying back to the old man's side.

Heinie's eyes stared unseeing. "Water!" he rasped.

"Oh, golly!" David murmured.

He knelt by the bed and put an arm under the slender shoulders. The old man weighed almost nothing. Gently he lifted him and held the cup to his lips. Heinie sucked greedily, blindly, like a newborn puppy. He swallowed, then seemed to choke. Yet when David took away the cup, he whispered, "More!"

Between them they spilled fully half of the water. "I'll get another cup," David said.

When he came back to the bunk he could see a change. A puzzled look had come into the little prospector's eyes. "Davy?" he questioned hoarsely.

"Yeah, Heinie, it's me."

"Davy, I am so sick!"

"I've brought you some water, Heinie. Do you think you can drink it?"

He tried to sit up, but David had to help him. He

seemed stronger after he drank, however. "Where is Blitz?" he asked.

"Outside."

David told how he had tricked the loyal young dog. "If you can keep her from tearing into me, I'd like to open the place up. This heat is pretty bad."

"Yah, it is in here like an oven. Yah, go ahead."

Prudently, David stepped behind the door as he opened it. Blitz dashed across to the bunk and actually moaned with joy to find Heinie conscious.

"Your telephone isn't working, I guess," David said.

At the sound of his voice, Blitz whirled and growled. Heinie reached a scarecrow hand out to touch her. "Blitz, it is our friend, Davy. For shame!" To David he said, "No, not for some time the phone does not work."

"I'd better go for help, Heinie. I think you need a doctor."

"Yah, you better call Dr. Hanson. I am terrible sick, Davy."

Before David left, he made the old man as comfortable as possible. Blitz sat beside the bed and watched his every move, but she did not growl again after Heinie spoke to her. She ignored the dry dog food David dumped in a pan for her.

Shorty must have thought a demon had lighted in his saddle. When David hauled him to a halt in the Wilson dooryard, sweat was running in rivulets from his gleaming sorrel hide. If the gelding had just climbed out of a dipping vat, he could scarcely have been wetter.

No one answered David's shout. He ran to pound on the door of the house and remembered belatedly that this was the Fourth of July. Probably the family was gone for the day. He could see a tractor parked in the equipment shed, and the doors to the garage gaped wide. The family car was gone.

He tried the door. The knob turned in his hand. He hesitated only a minute before stepping into the spacious kitchen and striding across the spotless linoleum to a modern wall phone. This was an emergency. With trembling fingers he dialed his home number. He couldn't expect Dr. Hanson to ride Shorty up to the cabin, but Dad would know what to do.

He waited, counting the rings. One, two, three, four, five . . . He let it go to twelve, then in despair broke the connection.

He thought about calling the Martzes, but they wouldn't be home either. Panic was gnawing at him when his eye fell on a neat printed card of emergency numbers taped to the wall above the phone. He rang his finger down it—Fire, Police, Hospital, Sheriff. "Sheriff," he said aloud.

Five minutes later David was on his way back to the cabin. He hoped he had done the right thing. The deputy on duty in the sheriff's office had sounded doubtful that Heinie was in as desperate condition as David described. A rescue by helicopter would be costly, he had argued, and so David had committed himself to cover all expenses in the event the call proved to be a false alarm. He had cited the reward money for Etonhill Princess Tanya. That had been the clincher. He had not mentioned that his share had been only one hundred dollars.

The copter beat him back. It was just settling to a landing at the mouth of Bootleggers' Ravine when he topped the hill. He booted Shorty into a gallop and joined the pilot and Dr. Hanson as they carried a stretcher up the trail to the cabin.

Blitz barked at their coming but subsided at once. Heinie was still conscious. "Take care of Blitz for me, Davy," he pleaded from his bed. "Promise me that you will take care of Blitz."

"Don't worry, Heinie. She'll be fine. She'll be waiting for you when you come back."

The doctor apparently already knew the nature of his patient's illness. He asked a few questions and made a very brief examination. "I'll give you a hypo, Heinie. It'll ease you some."

Blitz paced beside the stretcher when the two men carried her master to the helicopter. David walked along behind with a paper sack containing a few of the old man's personal items. He wondered if Heinie were going to die. He knew by the doctor's attitude that he had been right to call for emergency rescue.

"Davy, take care of our Blitz," whispered the old man. He touched the worried shepherd in farewell, and then they loaded him into the aircraft.

David backed away as the engine roared and the rotors began to turn. He watched the helicopter lift off and stood rooted while it climbed and swung away toward town. When he thought to look for Blitz, she was not in sight.

He called as he walked slowly back up the ravine. The dog showed herself in the clearing by the cabin, but fled into the trees at his approach. The thing to do, he supposed, would be to take her down to the Ittlesby ranch. He could not be riding up here every day to feed her.

He would leave the care of the cabin to the Wilsons, he decided. He'd have to call them, of course, but he wouldn't know what to do about the gas refrigerator.

He waited in the cabin for twenty minutes or so in the hope that Blitz would come inside looking for Heinie. Instead, the young shepherd took a position by the creek and did not venture near the door. Plainly she had no intention of entering the cabin while he was there.

"Guess I'll have to trap her," he murmured.

His gaze fell upon a ball of binder twine salvaged from bales of hay that had been fed to somebody's stock. "That should do the job," he said.

He tied one end of the twine to the doorknob, then laid out some forty feet of line so that he could sit in the shade of a fir tree and pull the door closed with a single well-timed tug on the baling string.

From her station by the creek, Blitz watched his preparations with interest. When he had taken his position and had not moved for many minutes, she stood up and slunk to the cabin door. Warily she placed her front feet on the big flat rock and lifted her muzzle. She knew that Heinie was not there. Even if she hadn't seen him taken away in the helicopter, her nose would tell her that he was no longer there. Belatedly, David wished he had thought to bait his trap with a piece of meat.

For a long, long minute the young shepherd dog stood at the door. As she hesitated David was struck suddenly by her classic grace. The thought crossed his mind that Tanya's ugly duckling was turning into a swan. Then she turned and trotted around the cabin out of sight. He waited, but she did not reappear.

"Blew that!" he grumbled.

He got food then and called, but Blitz did not come. As the afternoon sun dropped toward the ridges, he decided reluctantly that he ought to be heading back to the It-tlesby ranch. He put the food on the doorstep and closed the cabin door. Winning the young dog's confidence promised to be a slow process, he realized.

Dusk had fallen by the time he reached the ranch house. Link met him at the corral gate and offered to unsaddle and put away his horse. "Your mother's phoned twice, David. You'd better call her back. Where've you been, anyway? We were getting worried."

"Heinie's in the hospital," David said wearily. "I said I'd take care of Blitz, but I couldn't catch her."

Mrs. Ittlesby had his supper on the table when he walked in the door, but she suggested that he call his parents before he ate. "They'll want to know you're all right."

Mom answered the phone. The moment he spoke, she interrupted to say, "I've been trying to get you. The hospital called about five o'clock to say that your friend Heinie wasn't doing well and that he wanted you."

"I just got down from the hills," David said. "I'll come right in."

"I'm afraid you're too late. I'm awfully sorry, David. They called again about ten minutes ago. Heinie died."

6.

One-Man Dog

The day following Heinie's death was a Saturday. David had to work in the morning, but that afternoon he stopped in town to pick up his sleeping bag from home, and then he drove to the Wilson ranch.

"I promised Heinie I would take care of Blitz," he explained to Mr. Wilson, "but she won't come to me. If I have trouble making up with her today, would it be all right if I stayed overnight?"

The rancher offered no objection. "Heinie thought a lot of you. You just go ahead and do what needs to be done."

By the time he had hiked the two miles carrying his bedroll, David thought he would melt. He found Blitz lying in the shade at one end of the cabin. She sprang to her feet and challenged him, but plainly she did not consider the protection of her master's property as serious a duty as the defense of the old man's person. When David spoke to her and continued to advance, she circled behind him and stood muttering uncertainly. The food he had put out yesterday, he noted, was gone.

He stepped up on the big rock. As he opened the door, the hot air bottled inside smote him in the face and released a torrent of memories. Suddenly he had no desire to go in. He turned to look at the watchful dog and he shook his head.

"He isn't coming back, Blitz. He isn't ever coming back!"

He walked over near the creek and flopped down in the shade of a soft-needled fir tree. For an hour or more he talked to the young dog. Blitz gradually ceased her rumbling, but she wouldn't come to him. Nor would she wag her tail.

"Well, maybe you'll come for food," he suggested finally.

In Heinie's refrigerator he discovered some cooked meat. Blitz ate what he would throw to her, but she kept her distance. She had not forgotten that he had tricked her the day before.

"So, okay," David said.

When he fixed supper for himself, he did not prepare anything for Blitz. For the night he rigged baling string, running it out through the open door and back in through a window, so that he could close the door as he lay in the top bunk. Then he let Blitz see him place a pan of food on the floor under the table. Fully clad, he climbed up and stretched out on top of his sleeping bag.

Darkness descended slowly over the mountains. David lay perfectly still. He heard an owl hoot plaintively. A breeze whispered softly in the treetops, and tiny feet pattered as a squirrel scampered across the roof. He listened to the creek, its song like voices half-heard conversing in a foreign tongue. He waited, watching and listening, and after a while he yawned.

Moonlight lay in yellow rectangles about the room when a small noise awakened him. He blinked rapidly, confused at first as to where he was. Then he heard or sensed something moving in the gloom below him. The sleep mists vanished as he raised up and saw a dark canine shape darting toward the open door. Frantically he grabbed for the baling twine he had anchored to the bed post. His fingers brushed it, and he caught hold and jerked.

Even as he yanked, though, he knew that he was too late. Blitz was already at the doorway. Instead of blocking her path, the door struck her rump and added impetus to her flight. She yelped in surprise, and the door slammed shut behind her.

"Stupid!" David berated himself. "You've scared her now. She'll never trust you."

He shivered in the night chill. No point in opening the door again now. Blitz wouldn't be back. Disgusted with himself, he kicked off his shoes and climbed inside his sleeping bag. Within minutes a luxurious warmth stole over him and presently he slept again.

Blitz lay near Heinie's chopping block when he got up in the morning. He added some meat to the dog food remaining in the pan under the table and took it outside. The young shepherd ran at the sight of him; so he set the pan down and stepped away from it.

"Come on, Blitz," he coaxed. "Come on, girl. I'm sorry about last night."

She kept her distance, pacing nervously. He shrugged, finally, and went inside to prepare his own breakfast. Twenty minutes later when he looked, her pan was empty.

He wasted the whole day. No matter what he tried, whether he ignored the dog or sat and called and cajoled, the results were the same. She would not come within twenty feet of him or let him approach within twenty feet of her. She quit growling every time he moved unexpectedly, but she steadfastly refused to wag her tail. The exasperating part of her behavior was that she didn't really act afraid. Instead, she simply chose not to associate with him.

With shadows lengthening late that afternoon, David in desperation devised a new trap, or rather, a more elaborate trap. He ran the baling twine that he had used the night before directly across the room, from the window to the top of the stove, down the back of the stove, and out in front from underneath. To the end of the string he tied a venison roast, the last of Heinie's meat. He experimented until the door would close with little more than a tug. If Blitz attempted to carry off her banquet, she would shut herself in.

When he departed, he rolled up his sleeping bag and took it with him, so that there would be no reminder of him. He set no food at all outside the cabin. As he started down the trail, he looked back and smiled to see Blitz nosing about the doorstep. He had been cagey. He had pulled the door almost closed, but he had not latched it. She would think it had been left ajar by accident.

Heinie's funeral was Monday afternoon. David met a nephew of the old man, the only relative who attended. Heinie was buried in the local cemetery beside a brother who had died many years before. David did not return to the Ittlesbys' after the services, but instead drove to the Wilson ranch.

If his trap didn't do the trick, he thought as he hiked up the trail, he would ask a veterinarian about feeding Blitz some kind of knock-out drops. "Serves me right for not having gone to see Heinie more often," he told himself. "I'm a stranger to Blitz, and I should have been a friend."

When he approached the cabin, he could see that the

door was shut. He paused at the edge of the clearing to catch his breath and to listen. If Blitz were shut in, she was not protesting. However, just in case she was waiting to dash out when the door opened, he stepped to look in a window. Instantly the dog began to bark. She was there, all right. He spied her crouched on Heinie's bunk.

Although he felt fairly certain that the young dog would not attack him, his heart began to beat faster as he moved to the door. He listened as he lifted the latch. Grabbing a quick breath, he slipped inside and hastily shut the door behind him.

Blitz had not moved from her master's bed. In the low-ceilinged room her racket was deafening. David attempted to soothe her, and finally, out of desperation, he tried to imitate Heinie's accent. "Blitz, shut up!"

Taken by surprise, the dog fell silent, save for a low rumbling deep in her throat. "You're acting awfully silly," David told her.

He wondered if she would obey an outright order. Again in Heinie's voice, he said, "Blitz, come here!"

She flattened into the rumpled blankets, her dark eyes bleak with hostility. For the first time she seemed afraid. David knew better than to reach toward her, though. Fear could make her bite.

"Okay," he said. "There are more ways than one to skin a cat, or catch a dog."

He located a length of rope and fashioned a noose in one end. Draping the loop over Heinie's broom, he swung the broom into the lower bunk. Blitz snarled and sat up, but she could not duck the rope and keep her eyes on David at the same time. Deftly he slipped the noose around her neck and pulled it snug.

"Now, old kid, like it or not, we're going to get acquainted."

He set the broom aside and gripped the rope in both hands. "Blitz, come!" he commanded softly. Then slowly, slowly he began to pull. "Good girl. Good girl," he said reassuringly.

As the rope became taut, the young German shepherd braced her feet to keep from being pulled off the bunk. David set his own feet. Leaning against the rope a little harder, he intoned, "Good girl. Come on."

The blanket started to slip, and Blitz reared in a desperate effort to pull free. David was watching for just such a chance. With a single, well-timed jerk, he had her on the floor. "That's a good girl!" he exclaimed.

In the cave-like security of Heinie's bunk, Blitz might have defended herself, but on the floor with a rope about her neck she felt herself at David's mercy. Despite her size she was still, at eight months, only a puppy. Her toenails dug the floor as he pulled her to him; yet she did not growl and she did not bite.

"Good girl. Good girl," David crooned.

He gave no slack until her muzzle all but touched his pants' leg. Then carefully he released the pressure and with his fingers gently eased the knot at her throat. She trembled as he laid his hand on her head. Working quietly, he replaced the rope with a stout leather collar he had found hanging by the door and a leash he had brought with him.

"We'll get along, Blitz," he said cheerfully. "You'll like rambling around with Skipper while Link and I are building fences."

The young shepherd merely endured his handling. Her

tail hung straight to the floor as if weighted down by a rock. When the cabin door was opened, she attempted to bolt, but David was prepared. He gave slack, then set his feet and jerked on the leash with both hands just as she came to the end of it. Blitz yelped in surprise as she was flipped head for tail. "Good girl," David said quietly.

The lesson was rough but effective. Blitz did not lunge again. She had been tied up enough by Heinie to know the power of a collar and chain. Now she knew that she would not catch David napping. Head down, her magnificent stern drooping, she slunk meekly along beside him. Although he tried to apologize, she wanted to have nothing to do with him.

On the drive into town, with the dog in the back seat of the car, David considered exactly what he proposed to do with her. He had promised Heinie that he would take care of her, but did his promise mean that he personally would feed and house her to the end of her days, or just that he would see that someone took care of her? Dad had said one dog in the family was enough. Would he reconsider? David sighed. There was also the matter of who owned Blitz. She had never legally belonged to Heinie. Etonhill Kennels had paid a reward for the return of their champion show dog and given a bonus for the litter.

"I suppose I ought to call Price Sargent," David grumbled.

He passed a veterinary hospital at the edge of town and was jolted to realize that Blitz probably had never received shots for distemper and hepatitis, or rabies, or anything else. On impulse he slowed the car and turned to circle back. People who gambled with distemper nearly always lost.

Dr. Robles was busy with a cat, but he got to David in a few minutes. "This is a nice-looking shepherd, David," he said, when he administered the shots. "Where did you get her?"

Rather than go into a long explanation, David answered, "I'm just looking after her for a friend."

The veterinarian smiled. "That accounts for her unhappiness. These shepherds can be awfully one-man. I wondered at you, of all people, having a dog that wouldn't wag its tail."

A telephone rang and was answered by the office girl. "Doctor, it's Mrs. Wakefeld. She wants to know when you plan to look at her shelties."

"Shelties?" David repeated.

"Say!" exclaimed Dr. Robles. "You're a Shetland sheepdog fan, aren't you? Mrs. Wakefeld has a litter of pretty classy pups. She wants me to help her pick out her best female. Why don't you run over with me, David?"

"Sure!" David said. Nothing in the world appealed to him more. Then, thinking out loud, he said, "Oh. What should I do with Blitz? She's kind of wild, but if I shut her up in my car with the windows rolled up, she'll suffocate."

"Let Sharon put her in one of the cages for a few minutes," Dr. Robles suggested. "Sharon, tell Mrs. Wakefeld we'll be right over."

When David handed over the end of the leash, he had an uneasy feeling that he ought to forget about the shelties, but he shook the notion aside. "She's kind of wild," he repeated to the office girl. "Don't let her jerk away from you."

Fifteen minutes later he and the veterinarian had barely been admitted to the home of Mrs. Wakefeld when

the telephone rang. Mrs. Wakefeld excused herself to answer it, and from across the room David could hear the
high-pitched, excited voice of the caller.

"It's for you, doctor."

Instantly David knew the call had to do with Blitz.
Somehow he *knew*. He felt a numbness deep inside as he
listened to Dr. Robles' curt questions and sharp responses.
"It's Blitz, isn't it?" he asked as the veterinarian hung
up.

"Yes. She got away from Sharon. Mrs. Wakefeld, I'm
sorry. I'll have to come back another time."

On the way across town, the doctor explained what had
happened. "Some fellow came to pick up a dog we've been
boarding. Had a little kid with him. We don't encourage
the customers to come into the back room, but this youngster evidently followed Sharon. The first thing she knew,
your shepherd was out. Someone else came in the front
door just then, and the dog slipped outside before anyone
could stop her."

They arrived back at the veterinary hospital in a spray
of flying gravel. Sharon ran out to meet them. "I don't
know how she could disappear so fast. My brother is
cruising the neighborhood in his car, and I've got some
kids on bicycles looking, but nobody's seen her!"

She caught her breath. "I'm terribly sorry, David. She
didn't act up at all when I put her in the pen. I left her
collar on and just unsnapped the leash. But when that
little boy let her out, she took off just like some kind of
wild animal."

"Where's her home?" Dr. Robles interrupted. "In which
direction would she be apt to go, David?"

"She belonged to Heinie Wehring," David said, and

then he described where the old prospector had lived. "What scares me is that she's never been around traffic of any kind. She doesn't know anything about cars."

"We'd better alert the dogcatcher and the police and ask them to be on the lookout for her," the doctor suggested.

"They won't be able to get near her if they do spot her," David said gloomily.

He climbed into his own car, then hesitated with his hand on the ignition key. Which way should he go? Blitz would be frightened. Confused by the strangeness of her surroundings, she might hide in some dark cubbyhole, or she might already be two miles from town and still running.

Forty minutes of aimless patrolling convinced him of the futility of looking for the dog. He doubted, anyway, that she would come to him if he did find her. "Guess I'd better call the radio station," he decided aloud. "Better put an ad in the paper, too."

He arrived home as his mother was clearing the supper table. "Where's the dog?" Harvey greeted him. "Didn't your booby trap work?"

David got a fork and started in on some potato salad that remained in a serving dish. He told his story, making no attempt to hide his weariness and discouragement. "I just hope," he concluded, "that she finds her way back up to Heinie's cabin."

Marshall Hollis had wandered into the kitchen with an empty ice-tea glass in time to hear most of the tale. "Just why is this dog your responsibility?" he wanted to know.

"Heinie asked me to look after her."

"Just like that. How long are you going to look after

her? Who is it that's going to pay for the food she eats?"

"I'll pay for her food," David said.

"In other words, then, you intend to keep her."

"Well, gee, Dad, I promised Heinie. I didn't know he was going to die."

"Why don't you wire Etonhill Kennels? Wouldn't they take her back? I'd think they'd be able to sell her to someone else."

"I can't do that, Dad, when I don't even know where she is. If she gets run over or something, there'd be no point."

His conscience pricked him as he argued, but he didn't speak up. He had let his father believe that Heinie had bought Blitz from the Etonhill Kennels.

He called Johnny that evening, and after work the next day the two boys hiked up to the cabin in Bootleggers' Ravine. The jaunt in the coolness of evening proved pleasant but unrewarding. If Blitz had returned, she was careful to keep out of sight. David set out the last of Heinie's dry dog food and resigned himself to making the trip again.

The food, however, was not eaten, not the next day, or the next, or the one after that. Rodents fouled it and scattered it, and four days after Blitz escaped from the veterinary hospital a hard rain made mush of what remained. Blitz did not return to Heinie's cabin.

David offered a twenty-five dollar reward, but no one reported seeing the young shepherd—dead or alive. She seemingly had vanished. Then, toward the end of July, about three weeks after Heinie's death, ranchers a few miles up the valley from the Ittlesby place began to lose poultry to some kind of raiding varmint. The sheriff advanced the opinion that the predator was a fox or coyote. It covered too wide a territory to be a badger or skunk, and at the same time it seemed to be far too skillful and economical a killer to be a dog.

David was afraid to gamble. He contacted every rancher in the area and urged him to be on the lookout for Blitz. "Please don't shoot her," he begged. "I'll make it right for any damage she does."

Each weekend he borrowed Shorty and scoured the countryside. He could afford to pay for a few chickens, if need be, but he hated to contemplate what would happen if Blitz got into a band of sheep.

Toward the end of August, a youngster hunting rabbits in that area shot a coyote, and two days later a rancher killed a bobcat he discovered raiding his chicken coop. The evidence caused David to wonder if Blitz were even alive. Then that very same week a sheepherder grazing his charges on national forest land adjoining the Charles Lockwood ranch claimed to have seen the young shepherd. From the man's description, there seemed to be little likelihood of a mistaken identification, and David's hopes soared.

On the first day of September, in the middle of the afternoon, Mrs. Ittlesby drove down into the hayfield where David and Link were picking up bales. "Charley Lockwood just called," she reported. "He has a dog trapped under an abandoned building over on his upper place. He thinks it's Blitz."

David lost no time. Billowing dust marked the path of his Chevy between the Ittlesbys' and the Charley Lockwood ranch. As he careened to a halt in front of the rambling Lockwood home, a tall man wearing a stockman's hat and cowboy boots came out to meet him. When David introduced himself, the rancher smiled. "What delayed you, son? Come on. We'll take my Jeep."

The upper place was an abandoned homestead on a high bench a mile from the ranch house. All that remained of the buildings were a tumble-down barn and a one-room log cabin with broken windows and sagging roof.

"She's under the cabin," said Lockwood. "I was riding on that hillside above and just happened to see her duck in."

"If she spotted you, she may have taken off by now," David suggested.

"No danger of that. I rode down here to be sure I'd actually seen what I thought I saw. She was under there, all right. Wouldn't come to me; so I put a big rock across the hole. Don't worry. She's still there."

Stopping the Jeep a few yards from the cabin, the rancher climbed out and picked up a lariat from behind the seat. David had brought along a leash. As they walked over to the cabin, Lockwood pointed out a worn path leading to the hole under the old building. David noticed, too, the raw depression where the boulder that now blocked the hole had formerly reposed.

"This must be her den," he said.

"I'd judge so," the rancher affirmed. "How do you figure to get her out?"

David considered. "A pole and a rope might be safest, but I'll see. She knows me, even though she doesn't like me. I don't think she'll bite."

He squatted to grip the boulder. It was heavier than he had supposed, and he grunted when he lifted and rolled it aside. "Now to . . ." he began, but he broke off with an exclamation of surprise. A black and tan catapult had exploded from the hole. He had no time to think. Blitz knocked him off balance as she dived between his legs. He sat abruptly, the dog beneath him. Down they went in a clawing, scrabbling heap.

Blitz still had on her collar. David touched the leather, but he was unable to catch hold of it. Wildly he grabbed to hang on to the struggling dog in any fashion he could. She yelped as a wad of hair came off in his hand. Toenails slashed his leg. Then his fingers closed on her lovely, luxuriant tail. He realized he might suffer a torn wrist or worse, but at the same time he knew if he didn't hang on he might never have another chance.

Blitz sought only to escape. She made no attempt to bite. So great was her determination, she dragged David bodily across the uneven ground.

"Grab her! Grab her!" he yelled at Lockwood.

He couldn't hold on. The tail slipped right through his fingers. He heard a rope slice through the air, and an instant later Blitz uttered a startled yip. He scrambled to his feet. As Lockwood set his heels, Blitz turned a somersault at the end of the lariat.

"Whoa, Nellie!" exclaimed the rancher.

The young shepherd sprang to her feet and stood with legs braced. David attempted to speak soothingly to her, but he was panting so hard he couldn't talk. Lockwood burst out laughing. "That's quite a dogcatching technique you've got, son," he chortled. "For a while there I swear I couldn't tell who was tackling who!"

Blitz made no further effort to pull away. The rope had stopped her hard once, and she had no need of a second lesson. Unwillingly, she allowed herself to be drawn forward. Although she neither snapped nor growled, her dark eyes glistened with bleak hostility when David attached the leash to her collar.

"She knows you, all right," Lockwood observed, "but I wouldn't say she appears fond of you."

David shook his head. "No. She's a one-man dog, and I'm not the man. It may take some doing to win her over."

A lot of doing, David discovered. Blitz nearly starved to death that first week simply because she wouldn't eat. She sat at the end of her chain and looked with longing toward the hills. David hated leaving her tied up so much of the day, but school began on the Tuesday after Labor Day, and he had no choice.

Dad viewed the young dog anchored to the Hollis clothesline with increasing disapproval. On a Saturday morning as David was preparing to take her for a walk, he asked, "When are you going to write to Etonhill?"

"I've got to get her eating good first," David hedged. "They wouldn't be interested in a scarecrow."

Aside from his promise to Heinie, he would be ashamed to ship Blitz to Price Sargent. The sullen, half-starved pup was no credit to David's ability as a dog handler.

"She sure is a challenge," he confided to Johnny one day as they walked home from school. "She's smart. She learns real easy, but she won't unbend. She just won't wag her tail."

Johnny shrugged. "German shepherds are apt to be one-man dogs, I guess."

"Yeah," David agreed, "but after two months you'd think she could begin to forget Heinie."

"Why don't you take her back up to the cabin and let

her see that he isn't there any more?" Johnny suggested.

The more David considered the idea, the better he liked it. After school the next day, he loaded Blitz into his car and headed out of town. The Wilson youngsters were digging potatoes when he arrived at the ranch. "Sure, you can go up there," he was told. "There's nothin' there, though. We took and hauled ever'thing down here. Whenever a place stands empty, people go in and tear things up."

From the moment Blitz stepped out of the car, she was a different dog. She took a single startled look around and the aloof dispirited creature of the past weeks became a whining, pathetically eager puppy. She fairly dragged David to the start of the trail.

David almost wished he hadn't brought her. "You're going to be disappointed, Blitz," he said. "It isn't going to be the way you think."

His own emotions got rather twisted when he topped the hill and looked toward the mouth of Bootleggers' Ravine. Just about a year ago he had been lost in a snowstorm and had stumbled upon Heinie limping along toward home like a three-legged dog. The prospector's snug cabin had seemed a glorious haven that black, unfriendly night.

Except for the weeds at the doorstep and around the chopping block, the cabin looked little different than it had appeared the last time David saw it. Blitz strained ahead as they walked the last few yards. There was no lock on the door. David lifted the latch and rusted hinges creaked as the door swung slowly inward.

The emptiness of the room shocked both of them. The table and chairs were gone, the refrigerator, the chest of drawers, the bedding—everything but the massive wood range. A cupboard door hung open, and the smell of pack rats pervaded the stale air. Even the telephone was gone.

Blitz seemed stunned. Her nose must have told her long before the door opened that Heinie was not there. Yet, human-like, she had hoped.

David's heart went out to the dog. In other days when she had traveled the trail up from the ranch, Heinie had lived at the cabin. She had expected him to be here today, and the little prospector had betrayed her.

They stepped on in and David shut the door. Quietly he bent to unsnap the leash. "He's not ever coming back, Blitz."

Slowly she moved across the room, her toenails loud in the hollow silence. She sniffed the bunk and inspected a litter of torn paper and twigs on the floor. Wandering over to the stove, she ran her nose along its dusty surface. She poked into the open cabinet beneath the pump and sink. Finally, tail down, she turned in bewilderment to look at David.

"I'm sorry, Blitz," he said softly. Impulsively, he dropped to one knee. "Come here, girl."

He spoke in invitation. She knew the words were not a command. She stared at him, struggling against some force within herself. She whined. At last, crouching as if she expected a beating, she slunk to him. She trembled as he put his hands on her.

Exultation rose in David. Never before had she come to him of her own accord, not even to eat! Gently he stroked her and crooned to her.

He knelt with the dog until her shivering ceased. When at last he stood up, a sense of daring filled him. He wadded up the leash. Stuffing it into his pocket, he opened the door.

Silent as a shadow, she slipped out. He followed and turned to pull the door shut. In the moment that he waited for the latch to click in place, he wondered if the dog would be in sight when he faced about. Perhaps he had done a foolish thing.

He turned slowly. She stood by the chopping block, watching him.

"Let's go, Blitz!"

He started down the trail. He didn't know if she would follow him. He couldn't hear her, and he dared not look back for fear of alarming her. When he reached the edge of the timber where the ravine opened out on the flat, he felt someting brush his left leg. He looked down, startled. Blitz was right behind him, her long wolf muzzle almost touching the fingers of his left hand.

"Well, howdy!" he said softly. "Are you coming with me?"

7.

Moment of Decision

David had never known a dog like Blitz. Although she wagged her tail and obeyed commands with apparent good humor, she seemed to find no real joy in life. Underneath her surface cheerfulness was a layer of reserve David could not penetrate. She either would not or could not open her heart.

"I think she's waiting for Heinie to come back," David complained to his mother one morning. Dad had already left for work, and Harvey had gone to school early. "She likes me, but I'm just not number one."

Cleo Hollis wiped the kitchen counter top with the dishcloth. "Do you really want to be number one? Aren't you going to write to Etonhill Kennels about her?"

Johnny had let it slip one day that Heinie had never legally owned Blitz. With great reluctance, Mom had agreed not to tell Dad.

David shrugged. "I should, I guess. I just hate to think of her spending the rest of her life in a kennel. I don't think she could adjust."

"But she does belong to Mr. Eton," Mom pointed out.

"I know. I should write." He frowned. "Blitz is real funny, Mom. At Etonhill they'd feed her and take care of her, but what she needs is someone to love her."

Mom poured herself a fresh cup of coffee and sat down at the table. "I'm going to offer you a bit of advice, David. Don't get too fond of Blitz. Many people here in Winnegar already know or have guessed that she is Tanya's pup. The truth about her is bound to come out. Sooner or later she's going to be taken away from you."

"Yeah, I suppose," David conceded. "I just wish she would get to where she could accept people a little better before I let them take her."

He spoke of his concern to Johnny on the way to school.

"Why don't you put her in obedience class?" his friend suggested. "Remember how you bullied me about Shad until I finally took him to school? People don't realize now that he was ever shy."

David regarded his friend with respect. "Maybe that's not a bad idea. You were sure right about taking her up to Heinie's cabin."

He entered Blitz, accordingly, in a Beginners' course already in progress. The first instruction period he attended turned out to be a nightmare. Terrified of the other dogs and mistrustful of their handlers, Blitz snarled and snapped at anyone who came near her. Fortunately, the young man directing the class was able to recognize the difference between insecurity and viciousness, and seven weeks later Blitz graduated from the class with the second highest score.

"She could just as well have been first," David remarked as he took Johnny home after the exercises, "but she isn't interested. She isn't interested in doing things for me. I think she's still waiting for Heinie."

"I wonder what Shad is waiting for," Johnny responded. The collie had flunked the Open test again. "That show in Salt Lake is a week from this coming Sunday. Did I tell you I'd sent in my entry blanks?"

Without waiting for an answer, he continued enthusi-

astically, "Why don't you come with us? It'll just be Mr.
Harridge and me, and he was saying it was a shame no
one else wanted to go."

"Might be kind of fun," David conceded. "I'll think
about it."

He let Johnny and Shad off and drove on to his own
home. Parking in front, he slid from behind the wheel and
let Blitz out of the back seat. Fresh snow had fallen during the evening. He looked down the silent street and
breathed deeply of the cold, still December air. It was
late. The dog class final exams had dragged out a long
time. Most of the houses along the street were dark.

"Come on," he said to the waiting shepherd.

Many of the neighbors who owned dogs simply turned
their pets out the door to exercise themselves, but David
always walked with Blitz. He still had the feeling that she
might run off if she were just let out and forgotten.

Tonight, because he felt a need to unwind, he went
farther than usual. From habit, his legs carried him to the
high school. As he turned to go back, his attention was
caught by a light moving on the second floor of the old
three-story building. He frowned in puzzlement. No one
would have reason to be in the school at this time of
night.

"Must have been the reflection of a car light somewhere," he murmured.

He stood, unconvinced by his own argument. Presently
he saw the light again. It was a thin beam that darted and
jumped. "Flashlight," he murmured.

Who would it be, he wondered. The janitor? No, the
janitor would have a key for the light switches. A teacher?
Prowlers, maybe!

He realized that he himself stood out in plain view on the sidewalk, a dark figure against the snow. If some kind of unauthorized activity was going on, he was foolish to let on that his suspicions had been aroused.

"Let's walk on around the building," he suggested to Blitz, a delicious sense of adventure enveloping him. If the person with the flashlight was a teacher, there would probably be a car parked at the curb and footprints in the fresh snow leading directly to a main entrance.

The high school occupied half a city block with doors facing three streets. Except where David and Blitz had walked, the sidewalk in front was untracked. He turned the corner. No car at the curb, he noted. Fooprints going up the street, but none on the walk leading into the school. This end of the building was dark.

Walking on to the alley, he found tire tracks behind the school made since the snowfall. A light midway in the block disclosed no sign of activity, but the possibility of footprints leading to the back of the building interested him. He called Blitz close. If nothing else, she was good moral support.

Silence hung over the alley, broken only by the small, crisp noises of his own footfalls. One of the houses facing the other street showed a light in the rear, but even as he looked, the light went out. Near the far end of the alley he discovered where several persons had gotten out of the car. A jumble of tracks led toward a fire escape. He looked up swiftly, his heart pounding. The windows of the school building glinted like great blind eyes.

Trembling with daring, he walked over to the foot of the fire escape. Blitz accompanied him, but she refused to climb the iron stairs. The absence of risers seemed to frighten her. David didn't coax for fear of attracting attention. He didn't know exactly what he sought, but had some clear evidence of breaking and entering.

Halfway to the second floor, the fire escape angled across a window. Here all the tracks abruptly ceased. The window was closed now, but the snow had been scuffed from the ledge. Although David checked very carefully, he found no tracks descending the fire escape.

Like a frightened cottontail rabbit, he scrambled down the steps. As he darted out of the alley, he started to turn toward the corner, then checked himself and plunged on into the next alley. If the prowlers were to see him running across the lighted intersection, they might slip out of the school building before the police could arrive.

The second alley was dark, illumined only by the soft reflection of the snow. Several windows showed lights, but he shied from the thought of ringing a stranger's doorbell at this hour of the night, when his own home was but three blocks from the school. Then, halfway down the alley, he spied the black bulk of the getaway car. He knew from a hundred movies that it was a getaway car. It faced the far street, its lights out and motor idling. It was not even pulled over out of the traffic lane.

David's first impulse was to cut through the nearest yard to the street, but he mastered his fear. "Come on, Blitz," he said softly. "If we get his license, we'll really have something!"

When he strode closer, however, he forgot all about the number on the license plates. He recognized the car. The black Ford with a yellow fender on the left front belonged to a boy who had been expelled from school the week after Thanksgiving.

Uneasily, David glanced down at his left side. A small wave of shock washed over him as he realized that Blitz had stopped to inspect a garbage can. Too close to turn back, he started around the sedan. He could see someone sitting in the driver's seat. As he came abreast of the dark figure, a boy's low voice called, "That you, Albert? Where's the other guys?"

He decided to ignore the speaker. Albert Norgood was the owner of the sedan. In the dark, somebody had made a mistake. David had no doubt at all where Albert was.

Just then Blitz dashed from behind to overtake him. Immediately, the boy in the car said, "Hey, Hollis, where are you going?"

Reluctantly David halted. He could not very well pretend that he had not heard his name. "Walking my dog," he answered. "Who's there?"

"Sonny."

That would be Sonny Cleary, a sophomore who sometimes bummed around with Albert. David stepped nearer to the car. "What are you doing?" he asked. Not to act curious would seem suspicious.

"This is Albert's uncle's house. I'm waiting for some guys. They went in half an hour ago."

Sonny knew, of course, that the sedan with its yellow fender would be recognized. He had to talk to David in order to establish an alibi. Maybe there had been a light on in the house before he had parked behind the garage, but there was none showing now.

"Kind of cold to sit and wait," David suggested.

"I got the heater on. How come you're walking through the alley?"

David shrugged. "Just happened to, I guess."

"You headed home?" Sonny asked.

"Yeah."

David stood a moment. He didn't want to appear to be in a hurry. "I walk Blitz every night. She's chained up quite a bit. Well," he said, "it's getting late. See you."

The other boy did not respond. David called to Blitz and strode out of the alley. He had scarcely turned at the sidewalk when the idling motor roared to life. If David hadn't already seen the dark sedan with its yellow fender, he would have recognized the sound of its faulty muffler. Still showing no lights, the car leaped into the street and turned away. Skidding at the corner, it swung to circle the block in the direction of the high school. David heard the engine accelerate, subside, then accelerate again. On impulse he turned back to peer down the alley.

Sure enough, the sedan swung in behind the high school. Even as David stood watching, its horn blasted. The three sharp, closely-spaced notes were unmistakably a signal.

He did not wait to see how many answered the imperative summons of the automobile's horn. He had learned enough. "Come on, Blitz; let's go!"

He started on the run, but slowed as he realized that the boys who had broken in at the school would be long gone by the time he could raise an alarm. Even if he were to knock at the door of the nearest house, five or ten minutes would elapse before the police could respond to his call.

"Might as well take it easy," he told himself, settling into a brisk walk.

Minutes later he had just reached the corner of his own block when he again heard the roar of Albert Norgood's car. He turned as lights swept the dark street. The sedan shot toward him, and suddenly the beam of a spotlight caught him. Skidding wheels threw a spray of snow across the lawn as the vehicle jumped the curb and lurched to a halt.

Three boys scrambled out of the car to block David's path. "Where you going, Hollis?"

The speaker was Albert Norgood, a moon-faced boy with unkempt hair. At his heels was Sonny Cleary's older brother, Orville, and another older boy David did not know.

David's voice all but stuck in his throat. "I'm going home. I've been walking my dog."

"You got big eyes, Hollis."

The three sidled a little apart. David backed up. "I don't know what you're talking about, Albert," he lied, his mouth dry.

"You know all right, bright boy. But you ain't going to tell anybody. You're going to forget what you saw."

David took another step backward. He felt certain that he could outrun the three of them, but they stood between him and his destination. He disliked the idea of being herded away from home. He could yell for help, but the only light showing on this end of the block was at Mrs. Anderson's house. He could not expect much assistance from a widow in her seventies.

"Don't run away," said Orville Cleary. "We're not going to hurt you. Not really. We're just going to give you a sample. If you keep your mouth shut, there won't be no trouble."

"You shouldn't be so snoopy, Hollis," Albert said.

The third boy, fists huge in black leather gloves, flicked a jab that wasn't really meant to hit him. Instinctively, David dodged, and in that instant he decided he'd make a run for Johnny Martz' house. Johnny would be in bed, but he had an older brother who worked from three in the afternoon to eleven at night. Tom Martz would be eating his bedtime snack about now. With luck, the front door would still be unlocked.

David made his move so unexpectedly, he caught his tormentors napping. Unfortunately, he also surprised Blitz. He had forgotten all about the dog, and when he turned without warning, he stumbled over her. He exclaimed in dismay and she yelped. Unable to save himself, he fell headlong.

"Get him!" Albert said.

Desperately David scrambled to his feet. Blitz danced in front of him. He saw Orville Cleary coming at him and attempted to spin away. The toe of a heavy boot caught him on the thigh, staggering him. From behind came a clout on the shoulder that spun him half-around. A fist slammed into the side of his jaw.

As David tried to get his hands up to protect his face, he heard Blitz utter a curious groaning sound. Someone jumped on his back and bore him to the ground. He twisted, using his elbows, and fought free. Another kick dealt him a glancing blow in the ribs. He grabbed the kicker's foot and looked up into the twisted features of Orville Cleary. Beside him Blitz growled and the dark shape of her body rose over him.

"What the . . . ?" Orville started to say. His voice broke off as sixty-five pounds of German shepherd struck him full in the chest. He stumbled backward and went down. Over the snarling of the dog, David heard the sound of heavy material shredding. Then screaming rent the night.

"Shut up!" Albert hissed. "Shut up! Shut up! You want to get everybody out here?"

As he spoke, the bully aimed a kick at Blitz. But for the fact that she was in motion and already moving away, the impact would surely have broken some ribs. As it was, she emitted a startled yelp and turned eagerly to meet the new threat. Albert twisted aside as she came at him. Her flashing eyeteeth closed on the sleeve of his jacket and tore it from elbow to wrist.

"Atta girl!" David cried in delight. "Sic 'em, Blitz! Eat 'em up!"

All along the street porch lights began to snap on. Albert cursed and kicked again at the excited dog. He struck her a glancing blow on the head that served only to enrage her. Roaring in fury, she launched herself at his throat. Albert staggered and fell. In desperation he tried to beat the dog off with his fists.

"Call him off, Hollis! Call your dog off!" shouted the third boy. "He's killing Albert!"

"I'm bleeding!" Orville Cleary blithered.

"Help me, you guys!" Albert screamed. "Get him offa me!"

David lurched to his feet. Too battered to think straight, he knew only that he must not let his dog kill anyone. Albert meant nothing to him, but Blitz must not be permitted to earn recognition as a killer.

"Blitz!" he called sharply. "Blitz, come!"

The young dog did not hear. Or she did not choose to hear. Even as David stumbled to her, he heard the unmistakable crunch of bones breaking. Albert's shrieks of pain filled the night with sound.

Hastily David got hold of his dog by her chain collar. "That's enough, Blitz! Blitz, no! Good girl!"

He dragged her aside, and all the while she continued to growl and strain toward the prostrate bully. "Good girl. Good dog," David cooed. "Down!"

Reluctantly the excited shepherd obeyed. Trembling, still muttering, she watched the youth cowering on the blood-spattered sidewalk.

"Don't let go of him!" Albert begged. "He'll kill me!"

A door of a house across the street opened, and a man in a bathrobe stepped out to the railing of his porch. "What's going on over there? What are you kids up to?"

Just then the motor of Albert's sedan sprang to thunderous life. David looked up in surprise. While he had been busy controlling his dog, Albert's two companions had fled to the car. With a roar the vehicle leaped off the curbing and raced up the street.

"Why, those dirty rats!" Albert exclaimed, raising up to look.

A menacing growl from Blitz made him swivel in swift alarm. "You'd better sit still," David warned.

He turned toward the man who had called. "There's been a fight," he answered. "Would you mind phoning the police, mister?"

He called his parents from the police station to let them know where he was. He assured them that he was all right and not in trouble, but when the police cruiser let him and Blitz off in front of the house an hour later, he could see his father nervously prowling the living room.

Pride filled him as he strode up the walk with Blitz at

his heels. The police officers had had nothing but praise for the young German shepherd's decisive action in the defense of her master.

He stepped through the doorway, keyed up, bursting with the news of his night's adventure. "David, you've been fighting!" his mother cried.

"I thought you said you weren't in any trouble!" Dad chimed in.

"Well, I'm not. I . . ." David had forgotten until then his bruised jaw, and his clothes did look kind of rumpled, he guessed.

"You told us at suppertime that you were going to dog class. Do you realize that it is one o'clock in the morning?" Marshall Hollis thundered.

"Well, yes, I . . ." David started to explain. He could have gotten home almost an hour earlier, but after telling his story at the police station, he had waited to hear the report of the men sent to investigate at the high school. Since he had been the one to discover the break-in, he had figured he was entitled to a little curiosity. It had been interesting, too, to listen to the calls over the police radio as the sedan with the yellow fender was spotted and Albert's erstwhile buddies apprehended after a ten-mile, high-speed chase.

"I never thought to see a son of mine brought home in a police car!" Dad ranted. "Why didn't you come home after taking Johnny home?"

"I did, Dad, but I had to walk Blitz. That's . . ."

"Oh, good grief! Not dogs again! It's always something about a dog, isn't it?"

"Maybe, Marshall, you should let David tell us about it," Mom suggested.

"He can tell us about it in the morning. He needs to get himself cleaned up now and go to bed. Tomorrow is a school day."

Dad turned on his heel and stalked from the room. Mom looked distressed. "Who were you fighting with, David?" she asked softly.

"A kid. You wouldn't know him."

Hurt by his father's lack of understanding, David let resentment splash over his mother. "It wasn't important. I'll tell you about it tomorrow."

For a week the vandalism at the high school made headline news. In a senseless foray of destruction, Albert and his companions had caused over two thousand dollars' worth of damage. David and Blitz received full credit for the rapid solution of the case, but David's biggest satisfaction came from hearing his father change tunes. Marshall Hollis couldn't bring himself to say he was sorry for having jumped to the wrong conclusion, but he did admit that, "Maybe Blitz is one dog worth having around."

David could scarcely believe the change in his dog. In leaping to his defense that night, the young shepherd seemingly had hurdled some towering inner barrier. All of a sudden the great reservoir of love she had set aside for Heinie broke through the dam. In one lightning flash of violence she had given herself to David.

When Johnny and Mr. Harridge began making final plans for their trip to Salt Lake City for the December eighteenth dog show and obedience trial, David said he would go, then nearly backed out. He worried that if he left Blitz for three days he might somehow lose the key to her heart. At the same time, he realized that he needed a period of separation, a time to sit back and consider what he intended to do about a dog to which he had no legal claim.

"It's a shame you can't get papers on that dog of yours," Mr. Harridge said, the morning they started for Salt Lake. "I don't claim to know anything about German shepherds, but she looks to me like a pretty good dog."

David sat in the back seat with Shad and the Harridge miniature poodle. Johnny rode up front with Mr. Harridge.

"Yes, it's going to seem kind of funny going to an obedience trial and not have a dog entered," David said.

That was something else to think about. He would never be able to take Blitz into competition. Although the American Kennel Club would sometimes issue what was called a listing privilege to a purebred but unregistered dog, which would permit participation in obedience trials, David would live in fear that someone would be struck by the quality of his dog and begin to put two and two together.

The roads were icy in spots, but generally in excellent winter-driving condition. Reaching Salt Lake late in the afternoon, they found motel accommodations within a few blocks of the sports auditorium in which the show was to take place. Long before nine o'clock the next morning, when the judging would begin, they arrived at the show grounds. Collies were first up in ring one, and Johnny would spend an hour grooming Shad's gleaming black coat to luxurious perfection.

Since his dog would not perform until afternoon, Mr. Harridge went in search of some poodle people he knew from Denver. Left to his own devices, David wandered through the grooming area. He had not yet seen the show catalogue, but a German shepherd owner he had met in the parking lot had said that Etonhill Kennels had dogs entered in the show. It would be interesting, he thought, to see how Blitz stacked up against her relatives.

At moments the din of barking dogs was deafening in the huge low-ceilinged basement. There were dogs in exercise pens, dogs in crates, dogs on grooming tables. David saw a professional handler he recognized and asked about Price Sargent.

Busy combing a standard poodle, the handler jerked his head toward the far end of the room. "He's set up down there."

David thanked him and moved on. Some shelties caught his eye, and he detoured. A rather large tri-color looked good, but one sable had prick ears and another sable had scarcely any coat. They probably had been stuck in the show just to beef up the entry, David surmised. Points toward a championship would be awarded according to the number of dogs competing within the breed.

He went on. He came to some German shepherds, but they were not the Etonhill dogs. He studied them critically and decided they did not come up to Blitz for looks. Of course, you couldn't really judge a shepherd until you saw him move.

As he walked on down the cluttered aisle, a public address system blared to life. He spotted some more German shepherd dogs, and then he saw Price Sargent. He had never spoken to the Etonhill Kennels manager, save over the phone, but he had seen him on the Montana Copper Circuit. The pleasant craggy face and neat silvering hair had appeared in news photographs and dog magazines a thousand times.

The handler was in earnest discussion with a man whom David did not know. His assistant had a dog on the grooming table. At first glance David thought that the animal being brushed was Etonhill Princess Tanya, but it was a male, bigger than Tanya, and younger. David's interest quickened as he speculated that the dog might even be a litter mate to Blitz.

He stood back, debating whether he should make his identity known if the opportunity arose. When the assistant did not even glance his way, he turned to look at two other Etonhill shepherds. The first, a young female, paced restlessly in the small square of her exercise pen. The other lay calmly alert, a picture of regal dignity. Now that he actually saw her, he could not mistake her. This was Etonhill Princess Tanya.

"Hello, Tanya," he called softly. He wondered if she would recognize him. She hadn't really known him, of course. He had brought her and the puppies down from Heinie's cabin and kept them overnight, but the very next day had put them on the plane.

The champion show dog pricked her ears at the sound of her name. When David spoke again, she flopped her tail in polite acknowledgment, but she did not get up.

Behind David, Price Sargent said, "I want you to take a look at this bitch. I believe she's everything Tanya was at the same age."

David moved out of the way as the two men stepped toward the pen holding the young female. "She's a sister to the dog on the table," Sargent said.

"I like her head," commented the stranger. "Yes, indeed, this is a pretty fancy-looking pup, Price. How old is she?"

"Thirteen months. She won't give Tanya too much competition yet, but with maturity she'll make it rough for anybody."

"I'd like to see her move."

Sargent turned to call to his assistant. "Bring me a lead."

A man and a woman stopped to watch as the handler slipped a show lead on the young bitch and let her out of the pen. Gratefully David stepped over beside them. He knew his presence would not be resented by Price Sargent; yet he hated to stand there all by himself.

Sargent gaited the young shepherd up the aisle at a fast trot, turned, and brought her straight back on the same fast trot. David could not fault her way of traveling. She appeared to move effortlessly, back level, legs straight, feet close to the floor. The handler stopped her smoothly and posed her very quickly, very skillfully.

"I like her," said the man to whom the dog was being shown.

David did too. Anybody who liked a German shepherd dog would like this bitch. And yet . . . David would be the last to claim that he knew all there was to know about German shepherds. He judged dogs more by instinct than by acquired knowledge. He could see quality here, real quality, and yet . . . Blitz was a better dog!

The realization stunned David. He had known for months that to all intents and purposes he had stolen a dog. He had salved his conscience by reminding himself that she was the runt of the litter and couldn't therefore amount to much. But here was an animal that the experts said was good, and he knew beyond any doubt that Blitz was better.

"What did you say the breeding on this bitch is?" asked the man.

Price Sargent stepped away, and the young shepherd held her proud stance. "She's Tanya's pup. She's one of the litter that that kid in Montana saved for us. Her sire is . . ."

David didn't hear any more. This was the moment for him to step forward and say, "Mr. Sargent, I'm David Hollis from Winnegar, Montana. I still have one of your dogs. There were seven puppies in Tanya's litter, not just six."

This was the moment, and David let it pass. Trembling, almost sick, he fled the building.

8.

Good Medicine

School let out for Christmas on the twenty-first, three days after the Salt Lake show. In the midst of the holiday season, however, David knew neither joy nor peace. He had not spoken to Price Sargent. He had not listened to the small still voice of his conscience, and it had become a loud, insistent clamor. He had stolen a dog, a valuable show animal, and he could no longer deceive himself that she was a runt and a cull.

He knew what he had to do, and yet he hesitated. Actually, his motives were not entirely selfish. Blitz had to be considered, too. Some dogs seemed to thrive on an endless succession of dog shows. They were happy just to be fed and cared for. But Blitz had never been in a crate in her life.

Two days before Christmas, Johnny invited him to go snowmobiling. They picked up Link Ittlesby, who brought along a saucer sled he had borrowed from one of his little sisters. All day long the boys took turns being towed behind the snow machine while Blitz and Shad and Link's Skipper romped alongside. Blitz had never seemed happier. Truly the day was meant for boys and dogs.

That same evening a neighbor phoned to alert David to a program on dog obedience being aired on television. David tuned in and sat engrossed and miserable for nearly an hour. Painfully he searched his heart and soul. Finally, the day before New Year's, he reached the decision that he knew had been inevitable right from the start.

He spent most of that afternoon composing a letter to Price Sargent. He told the story of the runt that old Heinie Wehring had saved and kept for himself. He detailed his own involvement, his long struggle to win the young dog's confidence. He stressed the difficulty that Blitz would have in adjusting to anyone else. In closing he wrote, "I haven't got a lot of money, but if you will set a price on Blitz, I would like to buy her."

Then, before he could change his mind, he put on his jacket and strode a block and a half down the street and thrust the letter into a mailbox. Wouldn't it be great, he thought, if Walter Eton wasn't interested in the runt of the litter. He had been careful not to offer any opinion as to Blitz' quality. Since she had not been registered with the rest of the litter, there would be considerable red tape involved in obtaining her papers. Maybe Etonhill Kennels would not want to bother.

If he had hoped to find peace of mind through doing the right thing, he fooled himself. Even as he walked back to the house with Blitz frisking alongside, he began to have doubts. He felt as if he had betrayed a friend.

He figured his letter would reach its destination on Monday, the day after New Year's. The earliest possible reply wouldn't arrive before Wednesday. However, the telephone rang during the noon hour on Monday, and the long distance operator asked for David Hollis.

"Say, what's this about you having another pup of ours?" said the familiar voice of the Etonhill Kennels manager. He seemed interested rather than angry.

"I should've written a long time ago," David confessed.

"What kind of a looking dog is she?"

David knew what he meant. He meant, was Blitz a show prospect? He wished he could lie. He wished he could say, "Oh, she's kind of rickety, but she gets around pretty well."

Instead he said, "She's a good dog, Mr. Sargent. You'd never know she was the runt."

"You like her pretty well, huh, kid?" Sargent sounded sympathetic. "I tell you what you do. Ship her down to us and send along a bill for all your expenses. If she isn't something we can use, you can have her back for what you've got in her. How does that sound?"

"You won't be sending her back, Mr. Sargent."

"You're sure, huh?"

"I'm sure," David said miserably. "You'll take awful good care of her, won't you, Mr. Sargent? She's a funny dog. She's not shy, or mean, or anything, but she doesn't make up to people very easy."

"Sure, kid. We'll take care of her."

Certain details had to be discussed. Somehow David managed to finish the conversation. When he hung up, he knelt to hug the big dog lying on the floor at his feet. These days she was never more than a step or two away from him. Tears came into his eyes.

That same day he put Blitz on a plane for California. He wondered if he would ever forgive himself for shoving the bewildered shepherd into a crate and going off and leaving her.

The rest of the week he lived in a vacuum. He let himself hope that a miracle would occur, that Blitz would not measure up to the standards of the Etonhill Kennels. Then in the Saturday mail came a letter and a check.

"Don't blame you for not wanting to part with Blitz,"

Price Sargent had written. "She's pretty terrific. We'll keep you posted as to how she does in the show ring."

Johnny came over that afternoon. "Well, gee, David," he said reasonably, "they'll show her and make a champion of her. You couldn't afford to take her to the big shows, even if you'd had papers on her."

"Maybe Blitz didn't care about being a champion," David responded glumly.

His friend shrugged. "What'll you use the money for? Will you buy a Sheltie now?"

David shook his head. "Dad raised the roof when he found out that I'd known all along that Blitz belonged to Etonhill. I can't have a dog, not as long as Harvey has Muggins."

"That's a shame," Johnny said. Then he brightened. "If you'd like to just sort of keep your hand in, I could sure use some help training Shad. Hey! Did I tell you? My dad has to go to Portland on business, and there's a dog show the same day. If I can get Shad working, Dad says I can go. We'll be riding on a company plane, and it won't cost a thing."

David managed a grin. "Some guys have all the luck! Sure, I'll help you."

After school the next day they set up the dog jumps on a grade school playground. As they drilled Shad, a car pulled to the curb and a man sat watching them. They paid him no particular attention. Spectators had often gathered when David had trained Flash for Open competition. They worked without horseplay. Darkness comes early in Montana in January, and the weather, though not bitterly cold, was chill. David's toes were complaining by the time Johnny called a halt.

They were loading the jumps back into Johnny's car when the man who had been observing the training session stepped from his sedan and walked toward them. He was tall, heavy-set without being fat, a stranger to David.

"Hello, fellows," he said by way of greeting. Then, addressing David, he asked, "Aren't you the one who rounded up those kids who broke into the high school?"

"Well, I didn't exactly round them up," David replied cautiously. He wasn't just being modest. For all he knew, this man might be the father of one of the boys involved. He looked to be about the age of Marshall Hollis.

"But you are the one that has that trained German police dog, aren't you?" the man insisted pleasantly.

"I don't have her any more," David said.

"Did you train her yourself?"

"Yes, but . . ." David hesitated. "I just taught her obedience. She wasn't really trained to attack like that. She . . ."

"You ever trained dogs for other people?" the man asked.

"No."

"He could, though," Johnny put in. "His Shetland sheepdog, Flash, was high-scoring dog out of seventy-three dogs at Idaho Falls a year and a half ago."

"That so?" The man seemed to be impressed. "Could you teach a dog to track people?"

David nodded. He had never tried to pass an A.K.C. tracking test, but he knew the principles of teaching a dog to trail people. He had seen methods demonstrated at an obedience workshop, and he had taught Flash to find Harvey when his brother played hide-and-seek.

"What would you charge to train a dog?"

"I wouldn't have any idea," David said. "I guess it would depend what you wanted him trained for."

Abruptly the big man smiled. "Maybe I should intro-
duce myself. I'm Murray Williams, Deputy Sheriff. I have
a German police dog . . . Well—" he shrugged "—he's
mostly German police. Actually, he's a mutt. He's a year
old and he doesn't know anything. What I want to know
is, can you teach him to find people that get lost?"

Before David could frame an answer, the deputy continued, "Like last summer, there was that little kid that
wandered off from the Farmer-Businessman's Picnic. And
here a few weeks back we had that case out at the County
Home. If we hadn't just lucked onto that old fellow, he'd
have frozen to death."

"You can do it, David!" Johnny said.

The idea sounded fine. Here was a chance for David to
keep on working with dogs even though he didn't own
one. "I wouldn't know what to charge," he repeated, "but
I think it might be fun, Mr. Williams."

"How long would it take you to train him?"

David shook his head. "I'd have to see your dog. German shepherds are easy to train, once they accept you,
but sometimes . . ."

"That's no problem with Wolf," Williams interrupted.
"Wolf will love you on sight. He loves everybody. Look,
here's the picture, uh . . . I've forgotten your name."

"David Hollis."

"Well, David, this is the situation. I've talked to the
county commissioners about this. The county will make a
deal with me if I can show them a trained tracking dog.
How much do you suppose you could teach a dog in a
month?"

"A month?" David shrugged. "I could give him basic
obedience. That would include . . ."

His eye fell on Shad as he spoke, and inspiration came to him. "Hey, Johnny," he interrupted himself. "Why don't you run Shad through the Novice exercises. That'll show Mr. Williams about what I could do in a month."

They moved to the corner of the schoolyard to take advantage of the street light, and while Johnny demonstrated, David explained. "Heeling on leash is the first thing I'd teach him, Mr. Williams. Notice how Shad stays right beside him. He doesn't yank a guy's arm off, and when Johnny stops, he sits. He's not jumping on people and tangling the leash around their legs."

The deputy nodded. "You should see Wolf take me for a walk!"

Johnny took a moment to praise his dog, then posed the collie in a standing position. Telling him to stay, he stepped out to the end of the six-foot leash.

"Go and pat him, Mr. Williams," David invited. "This exercise teaches a dog to let a stranger come up to him. This is real important for a dog that's shy or one that bites."

The deputy sheriff walked over to Shad and stroked him. "What about a dog that jumps all over you because he's so glad to see you?"

"They're pretty easy to train," David assured him. "Okay, Johnny, show him heeling off leash."

Murray Williams watched attentively. "That collie acts as if he enjoys working," he observed in apparent surprise.

"With only a month to work in, your dog probably won't look that sharp," David warned, "but I could get him going pretty well."

Johnny told Shad to stay, walked about thirty feet away from him, and turned to face him. With a hand signal he called the collie to him, and with another hand signal sent the dog to the heel position.

"I'll teach your dog both voice commands and hand signals," David told the impressed deputy.

Now Johnny ordered Shad to lie down and again told him to stay. "Stays are real handy," David went on, "when you want to leave your dog in the car, or he has muddy feet and you don't want him coming into the living room."

"You can train a dog to do all these things in a month?" Williams asked.

Warm with nervous excitement, David shrugged. "I think so."

Thoughtfully, the deputy nodded. "Have you any idea how long it takes you to train a dog? In hours, I mean. I'd like to try to figure a fair price for your labor."

"For something like this," David replied, "I'd have to work the dog at least twice a day. Three times would be even better. The training sessions would be real short, though. Ten or fifteen minutes at a time to start with."

"Three times a day for a month," Williams repeated. "And you'll have to come to my house because the kids couldn't bear to be without Wolf for a month. Supposing, David, I would guarantee you fifty dollars? It would be worth that much to me to have him trained, whether or not we can interest the county commissioners."

"That sounds all right to me," David said. The offer sounded real good, in fact. His father ought to be happy if he were paid for training a dog.

Plans were made, accordingly, for the boys to go over to the deputy's house that evening to meet Wolf. David got home just as his family were seating themselves for supper. "Hey, I've got a job," he announced, swinging a leg over the back of his chair as if he were mounting a horse.

Dad frowned. "I'd suggest you go wash."

"What kind of a job?" Mom asked.

His voice rising with enthusiasm, David told about the meeting with sheriff's deputy Murray Williams. "If I do a good job teaching Wolf basic obedience," he declared, "then I'll get to go ahead and train him to find lost people."

"Hey, that'll be neat, David!" Harvey exclaimed.

Marshall Hollis snorted. "If you spent half as much time on your schoolwork as you spend on dogs, you'd be a straight-A student."

"Well, just because you don't happen to like dogs," David flared, "doesn't mean that nobody else appreciates them."

Dad shook his head. "Son, I do like dogs, but as I grew up I had to face some of the realities of life. And you're going to have to, too, some day. You're a junior in high school. Don't you think it's about time you devoted some thought to what you intend to do with your life?"

"Ah, Dad!" David muttered in disgust. Depend on his father to throw a wet blanket over everything!

Mom tried to smooth things over. Although she would never side against Dad, she seemed to understand the yawning chasm separating father and son. She asked questions about the new job, and David soon forgot his resentment.

He began to get cold feet as he and Johnny walked to the Williamses' home that evening. No telling what they might find. He might take one look at the Williamses' dog and decide he had made a horrible mistake. Looking back, he had set himself up as pretty much of an expert.

The front light had been turned on for them. When the

boys rang the bell, they could hear a dog bark. A moment later the deputy himself opened the door, and amid much commotion and shouting of commands, a huge black-and-tan shepherd dog plunged out. He was on leash, but he managed to plant both front feet in Johnny's mid-section despite the two small girls attempting to hold him back. While his pink tongue sloshed a wet welcome, his mighty tail battered the doorjamb.

"Well, hello!" Johnny exclaimed, and to Mr. Williams he said, "It's nice he isn't vicious."

"Wolf, get down! Wolf! Come back in here! Wolf!"

The big dog obeyed his master only to the extent that he diverted his attention from Johnny to David. David was terribly tempted to commence the training on the spot, but he stayed the impulse. He didn't know Wolf's owner very well yet. Right at the beginning Murray Williams might not understand the principles of correction.

Eventually the dog was controlled and the boys admitted to the Williamses' living room. "I should apologize," Mr. Williams confessed. "Generally when someone comes to the door, we shut Wolf in the bedroom, but I thought you should see what you're going to be up against."

Even standing still, Wolf took up a good part of the living room. His markings were those of a German shepherd dog, but his long legs, semiflop ears, and crisp, wavy coat suggested Wolfhound ancestry. If the long bushy tail could be believed, he was a happy-natured dog. Lively dark eyes promised intelligence.

"What do you think?" the deputy asked.

"I think he'll be fun," David answered truthfully. "If you want, I'd like to start his education right now."

"You're the doctor."

"Well . . ." In detail, David explained exactly how he would go about stopping Wolf from jumping on people.

Williams appeared eager to cooperate. "You kids stay out of the way," he instructed the two little girls and an older boy who looked to be about Harvey's age.

Johnny and David both went out the door as if they were leaving. Then, while Johnny waited on the sidewalk, David walked back up the steps and rang the doorbell. As Wolf sounded off again, he set himself. The door opened. Wolf lunged to greet him.

"Hi there, big dog!" David exclaimed. He stepped forward quickly. As if by accident, his right knee caught the oncoming shepherd full in the chest. His timing was such that the dog, his front feet already off the ground, was knocked over backward.

Wolf emitted a squawk of surprise. As he scrambled to his feet, David said, "I'm sorry, fellow. Did you get bumped?"

Instantly the big dog forgave him. He jumped up again, and a second time David flattened him. "Oops! I'm sorry, Wolf!"

Because David sounded sincere, the big dog could only conclude that the collisions had occurred by accident. He wagged his tail to show that he held no grudge, but plainly he had no desire to encounter such an awkward human being again.

"Good boy!" David told him. Then, turning to Mr. Williams, he said, "Johnny will wait a few minutes, and then he'll come to the door. It doesn't generally take too many lessons. If it's done right, the dog never knows he's been corrected. He just decides it isn't fun any more to jump on people."

Williams was impressed. "How do you do it? He's so big he almost knocks me down sometimes."

"Well, it's a matter of timing. Kind of like judo. You don't have to be real big." David grinned. "Johnny and I got lots of practice training Shad a couple of years ago."

The deputy looked at his dog standing quietly with all four feet on the floor and nodded his appreciation. "Sure beats yelling at 'em. By George, David, if you do a good job on Wolf, I may give you some kids to train!"

The next four weeks fled like autumn leaves before the winter wind. David never had a spare minute. Basketball took up much of his time. There were six-weeks' tests and semester exams to study for. And there was Wolf. He got up early to work the dog before school, worked him again after school, and generally managed to run over for a few minutes in the evening.

Johnny went to the Portland show and finally earned a leg in Open. He looked in the catalogue for Blitz' name, but none of the Etonhill dogs had been entered. A few days later David received a letter from Price Sargent. Blitz was unhappy and not eating as she should. Walter Eton had taken her out of the kennel and into his home in an effort to cheer her up. Was there any food, any particular treat, that Blitz especially liked? Any suggestions from David would be welcome.

David answered the letter, then tried to put Blitz out of his mind. Determinedly he concentrated on Wolf. The deputy sheriff's mongrel shepherd made an ideal obedience dog. He was happy all the time, and eager to please. Actually, he was good medicine for an aching heart.

Suddenly the agreed-upon training period was up. Williams expressed delight with Wolf's progress and asked

David to bring the dog to a meeting of the board of the county commissioners. "They've met my hound," he assured David. "I took him into their December board meeting when this brainstorm first struck me. They thought a tornado had hit. I think we'll show them something."

Just to play safe, David cut the seventh period and took Wolf for a half-hour run along a country road. A five-mile workout, he had discovered, was just about right to take the edge off Wolf's exuberance without unduly tiring him. When they arrived at the courthouse, he was glad for his bit of foresight. A whole crowd of men and women waited in the small meeting room of the county commissioners. What had promised to be a simple demonstration had all the look of a public trial.

Williams spotted him out in the big main hall and strode to meet him. "Don't be alarmed at the crowd, David," he said in an undertone. "All these people know Wolf and think they're going to see a circus. Just do your stuff."

Then, in a louder voice, the deputy said, "Why don't you bring him over here, David, where everybody can see him?"

The big dog had greeted his owner with enthusiastically wagging tail, but a tug on the leash served to remind him that he was with David. He moved sedately at heel to the open doorway of the commissioners' chamber and sat promptly when David halted. He looked around the room with evident interest, and his jaws gaped in a happy grin.

"Stay," David ordered quietly.

Letting the end of the leash fall to the floor, he stepped forward with Murray Williams. As he nodded self-consciously to the group sitting around the meeting table, he resisted the temptation to look back to see what the dog was doing.

"I don't believe it!" exclaimed a man standing by the window. "Murray's found a ringer for that big clown of his!"

"This can't be the same dog we saw in December," agreed another.

"How long will he sit there?" asked a handsome white-haired man whom David supposed to be one of the commissioners.

"I've never tried him for more than a few minutes," David admitted. "I've only been working with him about a month."

"Amazing," said the man.

"Folks," Williams said, "this is David Hollis. You'll remember that this is the boy who with his own trained dog caught the vandals who broke into the high school last month. David, I'd like you to meet . . ."

Embarrassed and ill at ease, David acknowledged introductions to the three commissioners, to another deputy from the sheriff's office, to a lawyer, and to various clerks and minor officials who worked in the courthouse. He knew only two, besides Williams, of the dozen or more people in the room.

"Okay," the deputy continued. "You all know my theme song. The county needs a dog that can trail and find lost people. David is going to show you what he has been able to accomplish in the way of training my dog in just one month's time. If you'll give us some financial backing, we'll show you a trained tracking dog."

Abruptly Williams turned to David and smiled. "Okay, it's your show."

David turned and was relieved to see Wolf sitting exactly as he had left him. "Well . . . uh . . ." he fumbled. He hadn't had much experience bossing a bunch of adults. "Uh . . . would you want to step out here in the hall? It takes quite a bit of room."

"Let's go, gentlemen," said Commissioner Ruebaker, the nice white-haired man.

Jostling and good-natured, the group filed out and seated themselves on the broad staircase that led up to the second floor. David explained and demonstrated the Heel on Leash, then bent with pounding heart to unsnap the leash from the chain collar. Sharply he ordered, "Wolf, heel!"

The big dog did a sloppy job off leash. His sits were crooked. He lagged on about turns and gamboled like a playful elephant when David broke from a walk to a run. The onlookers, however were not dog obedience experts. They were impressed that this overgrown pup they all had known would stay with David at all.

On the Recall exercise, Wolf looked better. David wouldn't have been ashamed to have been in the ring with him.

"Do that Stand for Examination thing," Mr. Williams called. "Like your friend did with his collie."

David nodded. He posed Wolf and told him to stay. Then, stepping to the end of the leash, he invited, "Someone come and examine him. You know, feel his muscles, sort of, like you're a judge, or something."

"Let me," exclaimed the lawyer who evidently was a special friend of Murray Williams. "That dog and I always wrassle when we meet."

Nobody could doubt that Wolf recognized the man.

David held his breath as the big dog threatened to wag himself off his feet. "Stay," he cautioned softly.

Wolf picked up one front foot and put it down again in the same place. He twisted his head clear around as his friend stroked him and thumped him in the ribs. But with the leash hanging slack, he stayed!

"You must have drugged him," said the lawyer with a disbelieving shake of his head.

For a finale David put the big dog on a down-stay and suggested that the onlookers try to call the dog to them. Wolf wagged his tail, but kept his eyes steadfastly on David, who was standing a few feet away. He did prick his ears with special interest when someone yowled like a cat, but even then he did not break.

"Gentlemen," said Commissioner Ruebaker when David had finished, "I'll offer this as a tentative motion. I should like to see some sort of agreement drawn up. Let's give this boy two months, or three months, or whatever it takes, and if he can train a dog to track human beings—and provided the dog is made available to the county, of course—we'll make adequate compensation."

"How about Wolf? Can he be trained to find lost persons?" asked another of the commissioners.

David nodded. He was ready for this question. "Yes, sir. German shepherds are used for avalanche dogs in Switzerland. They have very good noses."

"Everybody in favor say 'aye,'" joked the lawyer, who was not even a member of the board.

Lean fingers tightened on David's arm. "We're in, kid!" whispered Deputy Murray Williams.

9.

Imitation Bloodhound

Confidently, David plunged into his new assignment. Because he had taught Flash to locate members of the family in games of hide-and-seek, he figured that training Wolf to find lost persons would be a snap. He had a book that described how to train dogs for competition in American Kennel Club tracking tests, and he was all set.

By the end of the first week, though, David had changed his tune. Still confident, still enthusiastic, he knew he faced a long and rocky road. The A.K.C. tracking test, while not exactly simple, was mere kindergarten compared to real police tracking.

Fortunately, Wolf liked to play. The big dog would retrieve a toy as long as anyone would throw it for him. So it was an easy step to teach him to hunt for a hidden toy. David would leave him on sit-stay and walk around a corner of the house, scuffing his feet to leave a stronger scent. He would place the toy, then return to the dog by exactly the same path. Pointing to the ground, he would order, "Wolf, find it!"

From locating his toys in the yard, Wolf graduated to following a laid track that angled across an open field. At first David worked alone. He would walk out, drop the toy, and come back on his own tracks. If there was no snow to show him where he had walked, he would carry stakes and drive them into the ground to mark his path. In that way he could avoid laying confusing trails by accident.

In the beginning, the hardest part of field tracking was to teach Wolf to go in front of his handler while on leash. The mongrel shepherd had learned that his place was beside David. Now he was expected to forge ahead, actually to lean into the tracking harness that replaced his chain collar.

The weather cooperated. In the first three weeks, only two days were too bitter for working outside. Wolf soon learned to follow simple tracks laid by either David or Johnny. When he was reliable, the boys discontinued dropping a toy, and the track layer himself became the object of the search.

February slipped into March. Wolf made mistakes and David made mistakes, but the challenge excited them. Bit by bit the trailing was made more difficult. Finally Johnny could lay a track before school, and the dog would follow it seven hours later. Friends would pick Johnny up in the morning at the end of the trail and deposit him back at the same spot after school so that Wolf was never deprived of finding his man.

Toward the end of the month, a boy Wolf didn't know laid a half-mile track through the edge of town. By then the dog had learned to pay strict attention to business. When David put him on the scent, he ignored the distractions of other dogs and the cries of watching children. He led David through vacant lots and across a busy street. He lost the scent where it had been obscured deliberately in a gutter flowing full of melted snow water, but then he found it again and triumphantly trotted on to an automobile where the track layer sat waiting.

Satisfied with the dog's accuracy over a short course, David now set up a distance test. On a Saturday morning he took along Harvey and one of Harvey's friends, a youngster named Chuck, picked up Wolf and Johnny and Shad, and drove to the Wilson ranch. Carefully he explained to the smaller boys how to get to Heinie's cabin. "If you want to, you can go on up the draw and look for the old still where the bootleggers made their whisky," he added, "but don't mess around and get lost. Johnny and I will wait here for an hour, and then we'll start after you."

In his jacket pocket, wrapped in a plastic bag, David had an unwashed sock that belonged to Chuck. When the hour had passed, he took Wolf to the foot of the trail just beyond the corrals. Except for scattered drifts, the ground was bare of snow. He downed the dog and dumped the sock between his forepaws. Johnny waited a dozen paces back with Shad on leash. He had brought the collie along only to give him exercise.

Eagerly Wolf nosed the sock. In this manner he would fix the scent firmly in his mind. David didn't rush him. In a few minutes the big dog completed his inspection and looked up expectantly, his bushy tail beating the ground.

Picking up the scent article, David held it once more to the shepherd's keen nostrils. "Okay, Wolf. Find him!"

With a lunge that all but jerked David off his feet, the big dog took the slack out of the six-foot leash. Nose low and brush waving like a banner, he started up the hill on a trot. David trotted too. He would rather have walked and Wolf would rather have run; so they compromised. One thing about it, David thought; his wind had surely improved since the tracking program had started.

Because of a light breeze drifting the scent, Wolf ranged several feet to one side of the actual trail. The boulders of every size and shape that dotted the slope did not seem to bother him at all, but David had to watch constantly to keep from stumbling. Other than an occasional "good boy!" he did not speak, nor did Johnny. Talking distracted a dog at work. Besides, after the first couple of hundred yards, David had no breath for conversation.

Halfway up that first open hillside, a jack rabbit sprang up almost under Wolf's nose. David held his breath, but the big dog scarcely glanced up as the bunny raced away.

In the timber, the scent hung closer to the path, and the going was easier for David. Even so, he had to keep dragging back on the eager dog.

"Say, tell that imitation bloodhound to slow down," Johnny called from the rear, "or else let him tow me, too."

"Tow you?" David gasped. "I'm pushing. 'Tain't easy to keep this leash stiff, either!"

In time they came to the open flat on top. David looked ahead toward the mouth of Bootleggers' Ravine and felt an odd tightening of his throat muscles. He had buried Flash the night before he met Heinie. Now Heinie was gone and Blitz little more than a bright memory.

Confidently Wolf struck out across the flat. The wind was strong up here, and David noticed that the dog swung again to the lee of the trail. "Good boy," he repeated. "Find him!"

Without warning, Wolf stopped. He raised his head as if he had unexpectedly run out of ground scent. David halted behind him. This behavior, he had discovered, generally indicated that the dog had overrun a turn in the track, although here there was no reason for Harvey and Chuck to have turned. While he waited, David scanned the flat ahead for a flash of movement. He would not have been surprised to see a deer bound away to cover.

Wolf tested the air for perhaps a minute, then abruptly lowered his muzzle and began to circle. Puzzled, David gave slack. The big dog trotted a few steps in the direction of Bootleggers' Ravine, then reversed himself. All at once his tail began to beat furiously and he lunged forward again.

"Hey, he's going in the wrong direction, isn't he?" Johnny called.

"Yeah," David answered. He couldn't stop to talk. He had learned to trust his dog. Apparently the kids had disobeyed orders just to make things more interesting.

"Maybe he's on a deer track."

"Maybe. I don't think so."

Without hesitation Wolf headed out across the flat. His nose could "see" a trail that did not exist to human eyes. At a rapid trot, he led the boys in a great arc that carried them well beyond the mouth of Bootleggers' Ravine.

"He's got to be wrong!" Johnny panted.

David shook his head. He did not understand why Harvey and Chuck had made such a wide detour, but Wolf said they had.

In time the invisible trail curved sharply left. "That's better," David murmured, for Heinie's cabin now lay more than a quarter of a mile away over his left shoulder. As the track layers had circled back, however, they had dropped into a hollow and lost sight of Bootleggers' Ravine. They had changed course again as they climbed through a thin belt of timber. When Wolf crossed the main cattle trail around the mountain without a glance, David suddenly realized that the boys had headed into the wrong ravine!

"Wait a minute!" he said, hauling Wolf to a halt.

Some yards back Johnny stopped promptly with Shad. "What's up?"

"The kids are too far over. This isn't the ravine where the cabin is."

"Do you suppose they're lost?"

Before David could answer, Shad barked, and they heard Harvey shout. Looking up, they spied the boy running toward them from the direction of Bootleggers' Ravine.

"Wonder where Chuck is," Johnny said.

Harvey's headlong run slowed to a trot as he drew near. "Boy, am I glad to see you guys!" he gasped.

"Where's Chuck?" David snapped.

Harvey came to a stop and stood blowing like a winded horse. "I don't know. I waited and waited, and he never came."

"Why didn't you stay together?"

"We wanted to make it more of a test."

"He can't be too awfully far ahead of us," Johnny pointed out. "We've made pretty good time."

David sighed in disgust. "He's probably got himself lost. What do you think? Should we call to him, or should we keep trailing him?"

"Well . . ." Johnny shrugged. "We don't actually know that he's lost. Let's go on for a while. You wanted a real test for Wolf."

At mention of his name, the big dog whined. He could not understand the delay. If Harvey's appearance ended the day's run, then he was following the wrong track.

Reading the big dog's confusion, David took out the plastic bag containing Chuck's sock. "Here's your scent, Wolf," he said. "Good boy! Find him!"

Joyously, the big dog turned to his task. Within seconds he was on his way. Since there was no clear-cut stock path or game trail, Chuck had evidently followed a dry wash into the heavily timbered gash in the mountain. Wolf's erratic angling and occasional circling indicated that the boy had felt something to be amiss.

The terrain rose steeply. Here and there a tiny clearing opened among the trees, but nowhere was there a flat place for a cabin. "Gee," said Johnny, panting, "you'd think he'd have known he was in the wrong place."

David pulled up to catch his breath. The suspicion that their game might no longer be a game had him worried. "If we don't find him in about ten minutes, we'll start yelling," he declared.

A huge snowdrift, its surface made rock-hard by repeated thawing and freezing, lay at the upper end of the ravine. Wolf angled sharply across it and began to climb the ridge to the right. "Hey, he should have gone the other way to get to Heinie's cabin," Harvey piped.

"Yeah," David said.

They smelled smoke as they topped the ridge. Johnny caught David's arm and pointed to a thin gray streamer rising from among the trees in the bottom of the draw ahead. Turning to Harvey, he asked, "Did Chuck have matches?"

Harvey shrugged. "I dunno."

"Harvey," said David, his voice harsh with suspicion, "did you and Chuck cook this up together?"

"No! Honest, David! I didn't know he was going to get lost!"

"You'd better be telling the truth!" David muttered. "All right, Wolf, find him!"

The dog uttered a single short bark as he lunged forward. Almost instantly a cry rose from below, "Here, Wolf! Here, boy!"

"It's him!" Harvey exclaimed.

"Yo!" Johnny shouted.

As they descended the hill and threaded their way toward the fire, Chuck ran to meet them. Throwing his arms about Wolf's neck, the boy hugged the ecstatic dog.

"What's the big idea?" David demanded, masking his relief with gruffness.

"Well, our scoutmaster said we shouldn't keep going when we get lost," Chuck wailed. "He said we should stay in one place until somebody finds us!"

David realized then that the youngster had tears in his eyes. Chuck wasn't faking. He really had been lost. He had kept his head, too. His fire, built in a small clearing, was neatly contained by a circle of stones. With a stick he had scraped away all vegetation within a radius of several feet. He had built a safe fire.

David knew about a big boy who had been lost once. The big boy hadn't even been smart enough to carry matches.

To Chuck he said, "Lost? I didn't think Boy Scouts ever got lost!"

The boy sensed the softening in him. "Well, we do sometimes."

That evening, when David took Wolf home, he reported with enthusiasm on the successful man hunt. "I think he's ready to go, Mr. Williams. If you want to set up some kind of test, I think I can show the county commissioners a tracking dog."

Mr. Williams smiled. "How about showing me first? I

have tomorrow off. If you can convince me, next week is soon enough to put on a show for the commissioners."

They laid plans accordingly. The deputy's oldest youngster was camping with his Boy Scout troop that weekend at the Badger Creek campground a few miles from town. Williams said he would drive out first thing in the morning and arrange for a boy with whom Wolf was not acquainted to get "lost" from the campground.

"We'll give him a two-hour start and then call for you and Wolf," said the deputy. "I'll know where the boy has gone, but you won't. Does that sound all right?"

"Wolf will find him," David replied confidently.

Sunday afternoon he was ready and waiting when the telephone rang. However, instead of Murray Williams, Sheriff Bob Flagg was on the line. "Murray got involved helping his brother-in-law this afternoon. He asked me to fill in for him. I'll pick you up in ten minutes."

The officer had Wolf with him when he arrived. The day was pleasant for March, with the temperature near sixty. The warm sun and brisk breeze did not constitute the best conditions for tracking, but David made no alibis. He could not expect people to wait for certain weather conditions and a particular time of day to get lost. He had said he could train a man-tracker. This was his opportunity to prove that he not only could but had.

Sheriff Flagg was a short man, round-faced, serious. His quiet air of assurance had won him a reputation for being conceited, but David found him pleasant.

"I believe in the usefulness of a tracking dog," the officer said, taking the highway that led to the Badger Creek campground, "but I think that Murray should have had you train a bloodhound. A shepherd is not intended to be a tracker. They make terrific sentry and attack dogs, but they're not noted for their noses."

"Any breed of dog can be trained to track, though," David objected. "Even a bulldog with its pushed-in face has a tremendous nose compared to a man."

"True enough, but this is my point. I could take this car we're in right now and drive it across fields and over ditches. With luck and skill I might even get it on top of that hill over there. Why do it with a car, though, when four-wheel-drive vehicles are made for that kind of rough going? It's a matter of getting the right equipment for the job."

David had to concede the logic in the sheriff's argument, but at the same time he had utmost confidence in Wolf. He turned to the big dog, who took up the whole space behind the front seat. "We'll show him, won't we, feller?"

Snow lay in ragged patches across the campground at the end of the Badger Creek Road. Grassy slopes with western or southern exposures were almost bare, but timbered ridges facing east and north with their backs to the sun still wore their winter mantles. When the sedan, with its radio aerial and official insignia, coasted into the parking area behind the Scouts' tents, a dozen or more boys and their two adult advisers rushed to surround it.

"Understand you've lost a boy," Sheriff Flagg said.

"Yessir," said one of the men, grinning broadly. "Adam Jones. About two hours ago."

"Any idea which way he might have gone?"

A chorus of eager voices answered. "He was walking down the road." "I thought I saw him start up the trail to the caves." "He had a fishing pole."

Flagg played the scene dead-pan. "Have you searched for him?"

"Yessir, we've scoured the hills in all directions. He's not to be found."

Flagg turned to David. "Okay, son, you've got a typical situation. Everybody remembers seeing the kid, but nobody actually knows which way he went. For two hours now, they have been tracking all over the countryside, lousing up any possibility of a human being finding the right trail and probably goofing it for your dog. What are you going to do?"

David pulled in a long breath and released it slowly. His pulses were pounding with the same nervous tension he always felt just prior to going into the obedience ring. "First," he said carefully, "I'll have to have an article of the missing boy's clothing, something with a good strong scent on it."

"His things are in this tent right over here," said one of the leaders.

David stepped out of the sheriff's car and let Wolf out of the back seat. The big dog bounded over to greet his owner's son, but he whirled and came back instantly when he saw the tracking harness in David's hands. Trembling eagerly, he stood for the harness to be strapped in place.

"Okay," David said. "Let's see what we can use."

Respectfully, the Scouts stepped aside to let him through. The interior of the designated tent was a jumble of camping equipment, personal gear, and sleeping bags. "That's his stuff," said one of the boys, pointing.

David stepped inside. The tent had a canvas floor, high walls, a window. It seemed roomy. "This is his bed?" he questioned.

"Yeah."

Quivery with nervous excitement, David knelt to unzip the sleeping bag. He could feel the gaze of the sheriff upon him. Wolf stood beside him, head cocked with interest. Deliberately, when he had the bag open, David encouraged the dog to walk on it. "Down!" he said softly.

The big shepherd dropped and with audible snuffing began to examine the soft flannel surface under him.

"Now," said David, turning to the Scout leader. "I need an item of his clothing. A sock or underwear would be best. Is there . . . ?"

"He slept in that T shirt," volunteered the Williams boy.

Before David accepted the T shirt, he asked that the missing boy's other tent mates confirm its ownership. Wolf must not be condemned for failure because a wrong scent was given him.

"That's Adam's, all right," insisted the boys.

Using a piece of clear plastic brought along for this specific purpose, David picked up the T shirt without touching it. Wolf was going to need all the help he could give him. Today the dog must not only follow a track, but he must first find the track. Always before, David had given him a starting point.

While Wolf finished his inspection of the sleeping bag, David turned to Sheriff Flagg. "If this were a real case of a lost person and I asked you to clear all the extra people out of the area, would you do it?"

The sheriff nodded. "We'd cooperate."

"Well, then . . ." David hesitated. He didn't mean to sound like a show-off, and neither did he want to seem to be making excuses. "Well, Mr. Flagg, too many people following along distract a dog. I know these guys would like to watch Wolf work, but even if they don't talk, they'll bother him. Would you ask 'em to stay in camp?"

Groans of protest sounded outside the tent as news of the request was swiftly passed. Flagg nodded in approval and turned to face the clustered Scouts and their leaders. "This is official. Nobody follows us when David puts his dog to work. We have deliberately made this a tough test. Please don't make it any tougher."

As long as Wolf displayed interest in the sleeping bag, David did not bother him. Only when the big shepherd looked up and indicated by his attitude that he was ready to go to work, did David snap a fifteen-foot length of clothesline rope to the harness. "Okay. We're ready to begin," he said.

He knew the futility of asking his dog to pick up the scent in camp. Adam Jones had probably been back and forth across the camp site a dozen times that morning. The welter of trails would only confuse a sensitive nose. And no telling which way the boy had gone. Everyone but David knew, but nobody would say. Adam Jones might even have hiked straight down the road, just to do the unexpected.

Outside the tent David stood a moment, debating his course of action. The best bet, he reasoned, would be to walk out a hundred yards from the heart of the campground and swing a big circle in the hope of intercepting a fresh track.

"Was Adam out of the camp at any time before he got lost?" he asked. This was not cheating. He had a right to know.

The scoutmaster shook his head. "We stayed up late

last night, and it was noon by the time we finished our breakfast dishes. I'm sure he hadn't been out of the campground."

The sheriff hung back and Wolf danced at heel as David strode to a point below the campground and midway between Badger Creek and the road. Here David unwrapped Adam's T shirt and offered it for the dog's inspection. "Find him!" he ordered softly.

Wolf barely sniffed the article. He had already fixed the scent in his mind. Eagerly he dropped his muzzle earthward and began to quarter in search of the track. David stood still and played out the rope. He feared that Wolf might be discouraged if he failed to locate the scent he sought immediately.

The absence of a starting point did seem to baffle the dog. He searched briefly, then looked accusingly at David as if to say, "There's no track here."

"Good boy," David said quietly. Moving a dozen paces toward the road. Then he repeated the command. "Find him."

Again Wolf searched and again he drew a blank. David praised him and once more ordered, "Find him."

Stage by stage they crossed the road and plunged into scattered brush and timber on the other side. Wolf decided that he was not expected to examine every square foot of ground and began to move forward more freely. As always, the big dog was ready to learn a new game.

Nervous sweat made David unzip his jacket as he worked his way up past the campground. The Boy Scouts and their two leaders stood watching. Sheriff Flagg stayed well behind, offering no comment.

When he had made half his circle, David began to feel

trapped and a little desperate. Wolf sniffed at the broad Forest Service trail winding up Badger Creek, but he crossed it without stopping. Several times he paused to test vagrant air currents. "Find him!" David ordered softly.

Nose to the ground, the shepherd was trotting a zigzag pattern when all at once he jerked to a halt. He lifted his muzzle, pivoted slowly, then slunk forward as if stalking some unseen prey. David held his breath and stole along at the dog's pace, keeping the line slack.

Suddenly Wolf's tail began to beat furiously. He moved briskly in the direction of the creek, his nose skimming the cool forest floor. Even as David glanced back at Sheriff Flagg, he heard one of the Scouts exclaim, "He's got it! He's on the track!"

Adam Jones had crossed the creek on a fallen, lichen-covered log. When Wolf picked up the scent on the far side of the stream, he lunged forward with such enthusiasm that he all but yanked David, still balanced on the log, into the icy water. At that moment, David wouldn't have cared. He had proved to the sheriff that he had a tracking dog. The actual finding of the boy now would be duck soup!

The Scout had followed a game trail to begin with, but a quarter of a mile above the campground, he had re-crossed the creek and taken a stock path up a narrow ravine. His footprints made a dotted line across a snow-drift at the upper end of a steep, rocky passage. Then the ravine flattened, and the trail followed a shallow trough snaking up across a broad sagebrush-covered flat. Here the wind came at them from the side, and Wolf drifted far to the lee of the path.

David pulled up to catch his breath. "Pretty good bloodhound, huh?" he called over his shoulder.

Sheriff Flagg nodded. He, too, was breathing hard. "I'm seeing something I didn't expect to see," he confessed.

As they stood puffing, a small band of deer moved into view on a knoll a couple of hundred yards ahead and to the windward. The sheriff spotted them first and pointed without speaking. David counted seven head—no eight. Something apparently had scared them. They advanced in ragged formation by rushes and jerks, their heads held high and nervously turning. They seemed to have no awareness of the two men and dog standing motionless below them, and yet they wheeled suddenly and bounded around the hill and out of sight.

Wolf did not see the deer. David had chanced to halt him so that his view to the knoll was completely blocked by a clump of sagebrush. At a word from David, he resumed following the track of Adam Jones. However, when he had proceeded scarcely the distance of a city block, he abruptly swung about and halted with his muzzle high in the wind.

"He smells the deer," said the sheriff, halting behind David.

David frowned. "He doesn't usually pay any attention to other things when he's tracking."

"Maybe he's never run across a deer before."

With a whimper of eagerness, Wolf abandoned his old course to plunge in this new direction. His tail plainly said, "Hot scent! We're close!"

David was stunned. "Wolf, heel!" he ordered, his voice crisp with shock. "He's never done this!" he apologized to Sheriff Flagg.

Reluctantly, the big dog turned and came back. He moved to the heel position, but he did not sit. His great body quivered with the intensity of his desire to go toward the hilltop where the deer had appeared.

With shaking hands David got out the piece of plastic containing the soiled T shirt. "Here, Wolf, this is what you're supposed to be thinking about. Wolf, here!"

The shepherd whined. He wasn't interested in the T shirt.

"Looks as if you missed a few points in his training," Flagg observed.

"I don't know, sir. He's never left a track before, not since the first week."

"Well, send him on. We know he's been trailing downwind of the actual track. Maybe he just got off."

David nodded, but he knew better. Wolf's manner indicated a hot trail, not a lost scent. "Find him, boy," he said softly.

Groaning in his enthusiasm, the big shepherd bounded forward. He appeared not even to see the cattle trail when he crossed it. David pulled him up short and pointed to Adam Jones' footprints clearly visible in the soft dirt. "Here, you big dumb mutt! This is the trail you're supposed to be following!"

Wolf barely sniffed at the prints. He whined anxiously and tugged on the leash. Clearly, the only scent that interested him came on the wind.

"I'm sorry, son," said Bob Flagg. "Until those deer showed up, you had me convinced. I do think you've done a tremendous piece of work training a crazy clown of a dog, but you haven't quite finished the job."

10.

Tangled Trail

Disappointment sharpened David's voice as he ordered Wolf to heel. "I'm sorry I wasted your time, Sheriff Flagg. I really thought he was ready."

"I'm not sure that you did waste my time," said the officer. "Although I'm not convinced that Wolf will ever make a reliable tracker, I am convinced, David, that you know what you're talking about when it comes to dog training. I think that with the right kind of dog you could be a real asset to the Search and Rescue units of our local law-enforcement agencies."

David nodded in thanks. Yet no amount of sugar-coating could make the bitter pill of failure any easier to swallow.

"I'm sorry, son," Flagg said. "Shall we be heading back?"

"I guess so," David responded. "No!" he declared abruptly, "I'd better straighten this knot-head out, if I can. I'll catch a ride back to town with some of the Scouts."

"Suit yourself. I can tell you where young Jones was headed, if that will help. You'll strike a Jeep road a few hundred yards up ahead. The boy was to follow it to a farmhouse just out of sight over the hill."

David thanked him and they parted. Wolf still wanted to go in the direction of the deer, but David kept him at heel and strode up the cattle trail. He reasoned that if he hiked beyond the point where the deer had appeared, he might have a chance of getting the dog's attention back to business.

Wolf acted keenly aware of his disgrace. He slunk along with his tail down and ears back. "You big dumb mutt!" David scolded.

When they came to the Jeep trail, David tried again. He showed the dog the T shirt, then pointed to tracks clearly visible in the dirt. "Find him!"

Wolf wagged his tail in apology. Politely he examined the footprints, and then he turned to stand with his head high, his nose to the wind. His tail began to beat faster. He whined softly.

"Wolf, no!" Roughly David jerked the dog around and pointed at the ground. "That's the scent you're supposed to be following, stupid!"

The big dog cowered. The leash correction meant nothing, but he was crushed by the anger in his handler's voice. "Find him!" David repeated ominously.

Wolf flopped his tail in a humble appeal for forgiveness. Almost guiltily he glanced toward the rise of ground off to the windward. Suddenly brightening, he barked in greeting. David gaped in surprise as a boy appeared on the skyline. Obviously Wolf had known all along that somebody was there!

Even as he braced his feet against the big mongrel's excited plunging, David guessed the truth. This was not just any boy. This had to be Adam Jones!

"How'd he know I was up there?" called the approaching youngster.

"Is your name Adam Jones?" David demanded, sick with the realization of his own ignorance.

"Sure. I sneaked back out of sight to see him work. How'd he know I was there?"

David didn't answer. Not right away. First there was the important business of apologizing to a very intelligent dog! "Why didn't you show yourself when the sheriff was still with me?" he berated the Boy Scout.

"Well, I knew he couldn't see me. I thought he saw those deer that went running off."

"That's what the sheriff thought," David retorted bitterly. "He thinks Wolf flunked the test. But Wolf could smell you. He wasn't going to stay with a stale track when he had a fresh scent."

"Gee, I'm sorry," said the boy. "I never thought about the wind. Hey! Maybe if we hurry, we can catch up with the sheriff and tell him what happened."

They lost no time, but Bob Flagg's car was gone from the campground when they arrived. Dusk was settling when one of the Scout leaders let David off at home that evening. He meant to call Flagg right away, but he no more than stepped in the door than Harvey with Muggins at his heels ran shouting to meet him. "Price Sargent phoned, David! You're to call him back right away!"

David's fingers trembled as he fumbled with the zipper of his jacket. Why a phone call? Why not a letter? Something must have happened to Blitz!

Dad spoke without taking his gaze from the television screen. "I thought when you shipped that dog to California your business with Price Sargent was finished."

David shrugged. "I thought so, too."

Dad snorted his disapproval.

Striding to the phone, David was aware of tension knotting across his shoulders. In less than thirty seconds a stranger in California said, "Etonhill Kennels."

David identified himself and asked for Price Sargent.

"Just a moment, sir; I'll call him."

The "sir" made David smile. Anybody who had business with Price Sargent rated a "sir" from the kennel help.

In a moment the handler came on the line. "Hello! Sargent here."

David told who he was and asked, "How are you, Mr. Sargent?"

"Great! Say, kid, what I called about . . . we're having a dickens of a time with Blitz. She won't eat, won't make up to anybody, won't show—won't anything. Walt—Mr. Eton—got the idea you might be able to help us out."

"I'll be glad to if I can," David replied, warm with excitement.

"Fair enough. Here's the thing. We can't show Blitz; she looks like a scarecrow. What Walt wondered was, could we get you to keep her for us? You could raise some litters, maybe even show her for us."

Not in his wildest dreams had David conceived of such an opportunity. "You mean I could have her back and keep her here in Winnegar?"

"Yeah, that's what we had in mind. We'd work out some kind of financial arrangement. She'd still be Etonhill property, of course, and we would decide when she was to be bred and to what stud—that sort of thing."

David could hardly get his breath. "Gee, that would really be great, Mr. Sargent!"

"Well, look, kid, what about your folks? Should you clear this with them?"

"Maybe I'd better," David conceded. "My dad's right here."

Covering the mouthpiece, David turned from the phone. Before he could speak, his father said, "So they want to give her back. Or do they expect to sell her to you?"

"Neither one, Dad. They want to pay me to take care of her."

Marshall Hollis shook his head. "If you had your way, David, this house would become a kennel."

Just then Mom came from the kitchen. "I thought I heard your voice, David. How did things go? Oh, excuse me, I didn't realize you were on the phone."

"Hey, David," Harvey said, "do you really get to have Blitz back?"

"Is that Price Sargent?" said Mom. "What does he want?"

"He wants to turn this household into a kennel," Dad supplied.

"He wants to pay me to take care of Blitz," David said, feeling harassed. "She won't eat, Mom, and they want me to keep her."

"Isn't that wonderful good news!" Cleo Hollis exclaimed.

"Isn't it!" Dad grunted.

"May I say 'yes'?" David asked, quick to realize he had an ally.

Mom looked at Dad. "What do you think, Marshall? I've rather missed Blitz, haven't you?"

Dad sighed. "To be perfectly honest, no. How much do they plan to pay you, son?"

David shrugged.

"Ask him," Dad directed.

David hated to inquire. Etonhill had always treated him more than fairly. He took his hand from the phone. "Uh . . . Mr. Sargent, Dad wants to know what you had in mind to pay me."

Promptly the handler answered, "What seems fair to you?"

"Gee, I don't know," David responded. "Just to have Blitz back, I'd almost pay you."

"Well, how does thirty bucks a month sound? That would be over and above actual expenses for food, vet bills—that sort of thing. And we'd figure on a bonus whenever she raises puppies."

"That sounds great to me," David said. "Just a minute."

He relayed the information to his father, and Marshall Hollis shrugged in defeat. "I give up. Talk to your mother. If she's willing to put up with all the mud that gets tracked in and dog hairs in everything, I guess I can stand it."

"Oh, boy, thanks, Dad!" David glanced at his mother and caught her nod of approval. "Mr. Sargent, Dad says I can keep her for you. When did you want to send her?"

"There's a flight that gets into Bozeman at . . . let's see . . . eleven-fifteen in the morning. I can have her on Tuesday's plane if you can arrange to pick her up."

"I'll be there, Mr. Sargent. Don't worry about that!"

"Okay, kid. Thanks, and good luck. We're much obliged."

"Thank *you!*"

Turning from the telephone, David grabbed his mother and swirled her around in a wild dance of joy. "Blitz is coming home, Mom! I get her back!"

Muggins barked and Harvey cheered. "I'm glad for you, son," Cleo Hollis said. "Now let's all get washed up for supper."

In his excitement over talking to Price Sargent, David momentarily forgot about calling Sheriff Bob Flagg. When he remembered later in the evening, and telephoned the sheriff's office, a woman dispatcher answered.

"Sheriff Flagg is out on an emergency call," she said. Was there anything she could help David with?

He told her no, he'd call again in the morning. He thought Murray Williams would get in touch with him. The Williams boy would surely tell his father how Wolf had performed. However, Johnny was the only one who called. He asked about Wolf and was delighted to hear the news about Blitz.

Too keyed up to sleep, David lay awake long into the night. When Mom called him for breakfast, he couldn't seem to wake up. He had barely dressed when the telephone rang, and a moment later Harvey shouted, "David, it's for you!"

Johnny's voice came over the wire pitched high with excitement. "Have you looked at the paper yet?"

"No," David admitted with a yawn.

"Well, hey, there's a kid got lost up Homestead Creek. The write-up's on the front page. The sheriff's been out all night."

Instantly the mists fled from David's brain. "Yeah?"

"It's made to order for you and Wolf," Johnny continued. "Here, I'll read it to you . . ."

As David listened, tides of tension rose in him. He would go, of course. He would volunteer his own and Wolf's services. "You gonna come with me?" he asked.

"Can't. I've got that chemistry test this morning. I missed the last one and had to make it up. I don't dare miss this one."

"But, gee, Johnny, you've been working with Wolf almost as much as I have. You ought to come along."

"Boy, don't tempt me. I just can't!"

They concluded their conversation, and David hurried to eat breakfast. His father had already finished and was looking over the morning paper as he drank a final cup of coffee. David spotted the headline, MISSING YOUNG-STER, and by craning his neck managed to read the brief article. Johnny had left nothing out. Members of the local sheriff's force, Forest Service employees, and area ranchers were conducting a search for twelve-year-old Winston Grosser, missing since late Sunday afternoon from a rock-hunting expedition in the vicinity of Homestead Creek. Winston, his father, Winston's brother, and another man and his son had hiked up the mountain stream in search of moss agates. It was believed that young Grosser was carrying a .22 rifle, used previously that day for target shooting, at the time he became separated from his companions. Overnight temperatures in the area were expected to dip to 18 degrees above zero.

"What did Johnny want?" Mom asked, passing a plate of hot muffins.

"There's a kid lost in the mountains. He thought maybe Wolf and I . . ."

"Won't they call you if they want you?" Mom interrupted.

"No, the sheriff won't call me because he thinks Wolf flunked the test we set up. We'll just have to go and prove what we can do."

"You'd better talk to your father."

"Huh? Talk to me about what?" Marshall Hollis demanded, his attention wrenched from the newspaper.

"We were discussing that lost boy," Mom said. "David thinks that he and Wolf could find him."

Dad grunted. "Probably been found already. That article was written last night. And if he hasn't been found, they won't want a bunch of amateur detectives flocking in, getting lost, too."

"I'll call the sheriff's office and see if they've found him," David said, rising.

The same woman dispatcher who had taken his call the night before answered. "I'm sorry, the sheriff is out on an emergency call. May I . . . ?"

"They haven't found the boy, then," David interrupted.

"No, not at the last report."

"Well, look . . ." David identified himself. "I could go right up there with Wolf," he suggested.

"I don't know what to tell you," the woman confessed. "The under sheriff isn't in right now, and both deputies are taking part in the search."

David thanked her and broke the connection. As he stood debating his next move, the phone rang.

"David, this is Mrs. Williams. I don't know if I should bother you. I know you have school, but Jimmy keeps insisting that I call. He came home from Badger Creek campground yesterday raving about Wolf. Murray had already gone out on this call up Homestead Creek. Jimmy says you . . . you saw the story in the paper about the Grosser boy?"

"Yes, I was just wondering . . ." David began.

"Do you think Wolf might be able to help?"

"I don't know," David admitted. "I wish I could have known about this last night. The trail will be pretty stale now."

"Would you want to take Wolf and see what you can do? I tried to send word to Bob Flagg, but I don't think my message got through."

David glanced at his father. Dad would not like his skipping school. He took a deep breath. "I'll be over as soon as I can get ready, Mrs. Williams."

"Dress warmly," she warned. "When they called Murray yesterday, they said there was still quite a lot of snow in the higher country."

Behind David, Cleo Hollis said, "I'll pack you a lunch. You'd better put on your long underwear."

Dad looked at Mom, then swung his gaze toward David. He seemed almost to speak, but apparently decided he was outnumbered. With a frown of disapproval, he went back to his newspaper.

Mom was as good as her word. She had a knapsack packed by the time David was ready to go. "I made two vacuum bottles of cocoa and extra sandwiches, and I put in that old red sweat shirt. That boy is sure to be starved and cold when you find him."

David noticed that she had packed Harvey's knapsack rather than his, but he didn't say anything. He didn't really care, and he wouldn't have taken time to change in any event. "Thanks, Mom!"

She took him by both arms. "You be careful. No matter what, don't strike off all by yourself. I don't want you getting lost, too."

He grinned. "Not a chance."

At the door he turned. "Hey, Mom, if I'm on a hot trail

and I don't get back tonight, will you call Johnny and have him meet the plane to get Blitz?"

"You'd better plan to get back tonight," Cleo Hollis said.

He reached the end of the graveled road up Homestead Creek at midmorning. Only one car and a ranch truck with a stock rack were parked in the little clearing in the bottom of the wild twisting gorge.

"Looks as if we're too late," he told the big happy dog panting over his shoulder.

He felt horribly letdown. He had skipped school to make this trip. Surely, if he had met the sheriff's car somewhere along the way, he would have seen that red dome light and the whip radio antenna.

A man stepped out of the parked car as David drifted the Chevy to a halt. He was tall and thin and looked old. His hair under an old fishing hat was gray, and he walked with a limp.

David opened the door to get out. "Stay!" he told Wolf.

"Is there word?" asked the stranger.

David sensed both hope and heartbreak in the question. He shook his head. "I don't know anything. I was going to ask you. Is the search over?"

"Oh." The man seemed to wilt. "I thought perhaps they had sent you."

"No," David said. Was this old man the father of the missing boy? "I came . . ." he began awkwardly. "That is . . . I have a trained tracking dog. I thought maybe I could help."

"A dog?"

The clutching need in the man's tone jarred David. His

thinking all along had been in terms of showing what his dog could do, of demonstrating Wolf's value as a tracker. He had not thought about the people involved, of the boy himself, or of the family who loved him and worried about his safety.

"Are you Mr. Grosser?" he asked humbly.

The man nodded. "I'm Winston's grandfather. Is that dog in your car the one?"

"Yes, sir. He doesn't look like much, but he's got a real good nose."

"If looks were important, most of us wouldn't amount to much, son," said Mr. Grosser.

David decided right then that he liked this man. "Where's Sheriff Flagg?" he asked.

"Have you been to Cottontail Bench?"

"Cottontail Bench?" David repeated.

"Yes. They've established a base of operations there. Some of the searchers are carrying two-way radios. Reception is poor down here on the creek, you know. I'm stationed here just in case Winston should find his own way back."

David frowned. "How do you get to this Cottontail Bench?"

"Well, if you're looking for Bob Flagg, he's probably not there anyway. He'd be out combing the hills. But here's where Winston started. If that dog can follow a track, here's where you want to be."

David nodded. Mom had warned against his striking out alone, but what could he do? Here was the place to start, and time was of extreme importance. Each passing hour meant young Winston's trail would be that much harder to discern. He took a deep breath. "Can you tell me how far they hiked, Mr. Grosser? Winston and his dad and the others, I mean."

The old man gazed up the canyon. "Do you know this Homestead Creek trail?"

"No, sir, I don't."

Mr. Grosser turned and limped back to his car. "I've got a map. Did you tell me your name?"

"David Hollis, sir."

"Hollis?" Mr. Grosser paused with his hand on the door. "I thought you looked familiar. I've seen your picture in the paper. You're the one who trapped those boys who broke into the high school a few months back. Is this the same dog?"

"No, sir. This dog belongs to Murray Williams." David did not attempt to explain. People had gotten the idea that Blitz had been a trained police dog, and they didn't seem to want to hear the truth.

"Why didn't Bob Flagg call you last night?" Mr. Grosser demanded.

"Well . . ." David searched for the right words. "Mr. Flagg doesn't think Wolf is quite trained yet."

"He should have called you," Mr. Grosser said. "He shouldn't have overlooked a bet."

They discussed then how David should proceed. Although Mr. Grosser had not been along on the outing the day before, he had quizzed his son, Winston's father. With the map, he showed David exactly how far the rock hunters had hiked up the creek. In addition, he penciled in notations of landmarks that David might easily identify. "Sometimes it's difficult to judge distance," he said. "A mile on paper is apt to be two miles on the ground, especially where the trail follows a creek. You take this map with you, David."

While they talked, another car came up the road and pulled to a stop. A woman about the age of Cleo Hollis got out and came toward the Grosser vehicle carrying a vacuum bottle. She directed a wan, impersonal smile at David and addressed Mr. Grosser.

"Brought you some coffee, Dad. They haven't found him yet. Not a trace."

Mr. Grosser introduced David to his daughter-in-law. The young Mrs. Grosser did not look as if she had had any sleep in the past twenty-four hours. Dubiously, she regarded Wolf peering out the window of David's car. "There are almost thirty men out looking for Winston. Your dog won't be able to tell one track from another."

"He'll be able to tell, all right, if I can once get him started."

David explained then that he needed some kind of scent article. "I should have gotten word to you somehow," he apologized. "Would you have anything in your car? A glove, or anything?"

Mrs. Grosser frowned with the effort of thinking. "I believe there's one of Winston's socks. He stepped in that little creek . . . but that's been a week ago. You wouldn't . . ."

She walked over to her car, David behind her. "Oh, there's his cap!" she exclaimed. "He wore that yesterday morning. Would that do?"

"Don't touch it!" David said sharply as she opened the door and reached in. "I'm sorry," he added. "Your scent on the cap might confuse my dog. If Winston wore this yesterday morning, it should do the trick."

Taking a piece of clear plastic from a jacket pocket, he picked up the cap and carefully wrapped it. Excitement quickened his pulses as he turned back to his own car. He let Wolf out and swung the knapsack his mother had packed for him across his shoulders. The straps, adjusted to fit Harvey, had to be changed.

"If you see the sheriff, you might tell him I'm up here," he said. "He may think I'm trying to sneak in behind his back."

He put the tracking harness on Wolf, but did not attach a leash. "Not much point in trying to pick up a scent here," he explained to Mrs. Grosser. "I can save time by hiking directly to the spot where the other boys last remember seeing Winston."

Mrs. Grosser nodded. "I'm sure you know what is best."

Her voice sounded stilted, as if privately she disdained the help of a boy and a mongrel dog. Then, unexpectedly, she grabbed David's arm. He flashed a startled look into her eyes and was surprised to see tears brimming. "Find my boy, David! Please find my boy!"

"I'll do my best," he promised awkwardly. "Wolf and I will do our best."

Later, as he hiked up the canyon, his words haunted him. What if his and Wolf's best wasn't good enough!

He judged the time to be right at one o'clock when he came to an abandoned cabin about three miles from the end of the road. According to Mr. Grosser, the agate hunters had progressed only a little distance beyond this point. It had been on the way back to the car that Winston had disappeared. All three boys had run ahead. Fat, nonathletic Winston, however, had soon fallen behind his companions. They had assumed that he would drop back to join the two fathers. The men supposed, of course, that he was with the other boys. Nearly two hours had passed before the discovery was made that the youngster was missing.

David decided to eat. He knew that once he put Wolf on the track he would have little opportunity to satisfy his personal wants. As he sat on a sun-drenched boulder, sandwich in hand, he heard a motor droning overhead. He looked up and saw a helicopter angling like a big mosquito across the canyon. It looked like the same craft that had come for Heinie. He watched it idly and wondered if its pilot were still looking, or if the search had ended.

Finishing his lunch, he shouldered the rucksack again and attached a fifteen-foot leash to Wolf's harness. Thoughtfully, he strode toward the cabin on the creek bank. Starting the dog would be tricky. After twenty-four hours, Winston's tracks going down the creek would not be appreciably fresher than those coming up.

As always, Wolf was ready to work. David downed him on a snowbank where he could see that there were no footprints other than his own, and then he dumped Winston's cap on the big dog's forepaws. He allowed a good five minutes for Wolf to complete his examination before he picked up the cap and gave the order, "Find him!"

Scarcely a dozen strides from the snowdrift Wolf snapped to a point that would have done credit to a bird dog. Stealthily, as if he expected the scent to take wing, he crept forward. David saw the luxuriant tail begin to wag and knew the dog had found the track. Instead of lunging into the harness, though, Wolf glanced back at his handler. He had never before been asked to follow a trail this old.

"Good boy!" David encouraged.

Reassured, Wolf started upstream. This was not the direction in which David wanted to go, and when presently he spotted footprints in a marshy spot, showing that Winston had indeed traveled upstream, he pulled his dog to a halt. Here by the cabin, according to old Mr. Grosser, the three boys had been together, running downstream, headed for the car. Therefore Wolf was on the wrong track—the right scent, but the wrong track. There had to be another one going downstream.

On impulse he crossed the creek, stepping carefully from boulder to boulder. On the other side he found a path worn by fishermen. In it, footprints on top of footprints headed both ways. Many of these would be the tracks of searchers, he surmised. He showed Winston's cap to Wolf again and once more ordered, "Find him."

Many times in the next hour David wondered if his dog had any idea what he was doing. In the first place, Wolf was confused at being taken off a track and then being given the same scent again; and in the second place, traces of Winston's downstream progress seemingly had been all but obliterated by time and traffic. Yet apparently a track did exist, and by fits and starts Wolf worked it out.

At the confluence of Whitetail Creek with Homestead Creek, David met two men carrying back packs. He hated to stop to talk, but the two hailed him. They asked him if he had seen any sign of a twelve-year-old boy. "I'm tracking him," he replied.

The men looked at Wolf and exchanged glances with each other. "You're almost back down to the end of the road," one of them said. "I think your dog is kidding you."

"If he's tracking anything, he's probably following a deer," said the other man.

David shook his head. "He doesn't pay any attention to deer."

The first man identified himself as an uncle of the missing Winston. He had just driven over from Butte. "Maybe your dog's on the trail Winston made when he was hiking up the creek," he suggested.

"I don't think so," said David. That disquieting thought had occurred to him, too, but he reasoned that anyone hunting agates would have stayed right on the creek bank, perhaps wandering back and forth across the stream. This trail that Wolf followed seemed fairly direct, like a homeward path.

He wanted to ask the two men to accompany him, but the possibility of failure made him hesitate. If Wolf *had* goofed, who needed an audience?

"We'd better get going," the second man said. "There's a cabin at the head of Whitetail. He may have taken refuge there."

They had started on when Winston's uncle turned abruptly. "Say, kid, you haven't got some matches on you? We've only got a book between us."

David felt in his jacket pocket. He had kitchen matches in a small glass bottle and a packet of book matches. "Here, you can take all of them," he said. "I have more in my rucksack."

When the two men had gone, he checked his map. Whitetail Creek dumped into Homestead Creek less than half a mile above the end of the road. The realization that he was that close to his car jarred him. Yet, if he had learned anything these past few days, he had learned he must not doubt his dog.

Ordered to proceed, Wolf continued downstream. Several times he stopped, as if baffled by conflicting trails, but each time he moved on in the same direction. David began to worry in spite of his resolve to trust the dog. Supposing that Winston Grosser had not been interested in finding agates, wasn't it possible that the boy had followed his companions up the creek by the easiest and most direct route and that Wolf had been back-trailing this whole distance?

David hated to think about disappointing Winston's mother and old Mr. Grosser.

All at once the leash went slack as Wolf overran a turn and circled to relocate the scent. David stood still, then grunted in surprise as the dog struck off at right angles to his old course. At this point Winston evidently had turned directly away from the creek.

"Good boy!" David cried softly.

Confidently Wolf leaned into his harness. He followed a game trail that climbed a timbered hillside. Once on top, he trotted briskly out across a tiny mountain meadow. At the foot of a second rise, a huge snowdrift lay among the trees, and across it angled a string of footprints grown large in the mid-day sun. David paused to catch his breath and to praise a certain mongrel shepherd that need never take a back seat to any bloodhound.

Climbing again, they came to another meadow. Here the trail turned sharply without apparent reason, and after a while David became aware of spatters of bright red in the dead winter grass.

"Looks like blood," he muttered in puzzlement.

His first thought was that Winston had somehow hurt himself. Then he wondered if Wolf had swerved from man-tracking to trailing some kind of injured wild game. Not for several minutes did he remember that Winston was supposed to be carrying a .22 rifle.

"He's potted something," he murmured in sudden comprehension.

He watched closely, and in the mud of a forest trail he found deer tracks. Later he discovered where the deer had stood and bled, and he saw boy-sized tracks there ahead of his own. Evidently after wounding the deer, Winston had followed the trail of blood spots.

"Crazy kid!" David muttered. "He must know it's illegal to shoot a deer this time of year."

The track led on and on, now climbing, now descending. David stopped every so often to study his map, but he hadn't had much experience reading a contour map. Besides, he had no compass. Oh, well, he thought, if he got lost he could always walk downhill until he got to somewhere. Heinie had told him that.

The very fact, though, that he considered the possibility of getting lost sharpened his awareness of Winston's situation. The boy had followed the bloody trail of the deer, very likely without paying much attention to where he was going. Presently the sun had slipped behind the mountain and dusk had been upon him almost before he realized.

"I'm doing the same thing!" David exclaimed in sudden concern. The afternoon had fled away. Even now the sun dipped toward the ridges.

A breeze sprang up. As Wolf drifted downwind of the

actual track, David hoped the dog was still following the boy and had not switched to the blood scent of the deer. Then he spied Winston's tracks curving down a big drift, and Wolf swung, too.

Somewhere along the way they lost contact with the deer's trail. From the aimless turning and angling of Winston's path, David deduced that the boy had at last become aware that he was lost.

Atop a boulder-studded ridge, Wolf came to a halt. He lifted his muzzle to test the air rising from a canyon beyond. David saw him stiffen to attention and heard the strange cry of excitement that was neither whine nor bark. Before he could react, the big dog lunged ahead and yanked the leash from his hand.

"Hey!" David yelped.

Something popped. The sound had a flat quality like a paper bag blown up and smashed. David stared in disbelief as Wolf cart-wheeled heels over head and fell inert against a jutting slab of stone. Belatedly David realized that the report had been a gunshot.

11.

Smoke Signal

David knew at once who had fired the shot. "You chowder-head!" he shouted. "Why don't you look at what you're shooting!"

Instantly, from a jumble of rock fifty yards down the slope, a girlish-sounding voice wailed, "Help!"

Anybody who could still shoot and still yell couldn't be too bad off. David ran to Wolf. The big mongrel lay sprawled in a lifeless heap. On the top of his neck, just forward of the shoulders, a glistening red stain widened slowly.

"Help me! I'm down here!" Winston Grosser cried wretchedly.

"Oh, shut up!" David shouted back.

As he knelt by the great slack body, a quiver rippled along one powerful foreleg. Wolf lived!

"I'm sorry, mister," Winston called. "I didn't know he was a dog. I thought he was a wolf."

Sounding more human than canine, Wolf groaned. David leaned close to croon encouragement, and the bushy tail flopped feebly. In a few seconds the big dog was able to struggle to his feet. He stood swaying drunk-enly. "Easy, ol' kid," David murmured.

Apparently the bullet had just grazed the spine. Al-ready the flow of blood seemed to be slackening. "Dumb kid!" David grumbled. "Shouldn't have been turned loose with a gun in the first place!"

When he was sure that Wolf was going to be all right, he strode down the slope toward the pile of rocks where Winston waited. Only then, with the chill of night settling over the mountains, did he think to wonder why Winston had not run to join him.

"Are you hurt, kid?" he called, ashamed suddenly of his indifference.

"My knee is hurt."

Winston was not only tall for a twelve-year-old, but he was built like a tank. David's first impression of the boy he found huddled in a hollow among the rocks was that in about four years he would make a terrific football player. "Hi, Winston," he said, "I'm sorry I yelled at you the way I did. I got pretty upset when I thought you'd killed my dog."

"How come you know my name?"

David hopped down to the boy's level. "You're famous. Everybody's looking for you. I'm David Hollis. My dizzy partner here is Wolf. You'd better thank him for finding you."

Wolf half-fell, half-jumped as he joined them in the hollow. If he was aware that this boy had caused his hurt, he bore no resentment. His ever-happy tail threatened to disrupt his balance completely.

"Gee, he's big!" Winston said. "Hello, dog. Honest, I thought he was a wolf."

The boy sat with his legs out in front of him. David could see that the fabric of his jeans around his left knee was stretched unnaturally tight. "What happened?" he asked.

"I fell. I crawled down in here because it's out of the wind."

"Haven't you even had a fire?" David marveled.

It was a dumb question. The bare rocks afforded no fuel for a fire. "How long have you been here, Winston?"

"Since last night. I got scared when it started to get dark. I was running, and I fell. Do you have anything to eat?"

David exclaimed at his thoughtlessness. Shedding his pack, he pulled out sandwiches and a candy bar. "There's a Thermos of cocoa in here, too," he said. "Are you cold?"

That was a foolish question, too. The boy's lips were blue. His bare hands would scarcely function to unwrap the sandwiches.

Hastily, David dug out the sweat shirt his mother had packed and Winston's cap. "Here, put these on. Let me hold the sandwiches."

His mouth watered at the smell of canned tuna fish. He had worked up a fair appetite himself. No time to eat now, though, he thought. Better pick out a camp site and get a fire built while he still had daylight.

Confidently, he rummaged in the knapsack. He always carried kitchen matches in a waterproof container and book matches. He frowned when he encountered neither. Carefully he pulled out the rest of the sandwiches, two oranges, and three more candy bars. A length of clothes-line rope reposed in the bottom of the pack, and that was all. In sudden alarm he dumped the knapsack upside down. A marble dropped out, but no matches appeared.

Suddenly he remembered. This was Harvey's knapsack. The matches were home in his own equipment! In alarm he pawed through his pockets. He hadn't a match to his name. He had given all that he had to Winston's uncle and the other man.

"What's the matter?" Winston asked, his mouth full.

"Have you got any matches?" David demanded.

"Haven't you?"

Too shocked to think, David could only sigh. Talk about stupid!

In sympathy—or was it hunger?—Wolf nuzzled his limp fingers. David looked down and the dog glanced hopefully at the sandwiches piled within easy reach on a flat rock. David groaned. He hadn't brought along any dog food. Apparently he hadn't thought about a lot of things. Instead of rescuing Winston Grosser, all he'd managed to do so far was get lost with him.

"Better slow down on those sandwiches," he advised gruffly as the boy reached for a second package. "We may need 'em worse later. Here, eat the candy bar. Wolf, you wait."

He straightened to full height, debating his next course of action. Winston's hollow in the rocks offered no space to lie down and promised cold sitting through the long hours of night. "There's timber just below here," he said thoughtfully. "Believe I'll hike down and take a look."

Winston jerked to attention. "Don't leave me!"

"I'll come back."

Wolf followed him down the slope. The big shepherd seemed to be all right but didn't act very peppy. "Boy, what a mess!" David muttered.

With daylight rapidly waning he found a shelter—a cavity at the base of a rock ledge protected by a huge fir tree. He spied it from above and dropped down. A deep layer of evergreen needles made the ground seem soft. The wind did not reach in through the dense boughs of the tree.

Quickly he climbed back up the slope. He could hear Winston calling to him, and he answered. He didn't much blame the boy for not wanting to spend another night alone on the mountain.

The youngster had finished eating and stuffed things back into the knapsack. "I've found a place," David told him. "Can you walk at all?"

Winston shook his head, the motion barely visible in the deepening dusk. "My knee hurts too much."

"It isn't very far," David said. "If I help you, maybe you can hop on your good leg."

"I don't think so," Winston whimpered.

"You've got to try. It's too cold to stay up here," David argued.

"I can't!"

"Oh, sure you can. Come on, it's getting dark."

Probably the youngster's knee did hurt, but David was tired and in a hurry, and his patience wore thin. Winston wouldn't make any effort. He finally put one arm over David's shoulder, but he wouldn't attempt to hobble on his good leg. In disgust David finally offered to carry him piggyback.

"I don't think I can," Winston wailed.

"Oh, for Pete's sake!" David muttered.

Winston weighed very nearly as much as he did, but he managed to lug him to the shelter he had found. "Crawl in," he ordered, "and start breaking off tips for a bough bed. I'll go get my knapsack and the rifle."

"Don't leave me, David!"

"You'll be all right."

When he returned, Winston had not moved an inch. David almost fell over him in the darkness. "Come on,

Winston," he encouraged. "It's real nice in there back of the tree."

"I'm cold!"

"If you'd move around a little, you wouldn't be so cold."

"I wish we had a fire," Winston said.

"I wish we were home," David retorted.

"Do you know how to get home, David?"

"Sure," David lied. "I can't carry you, though. We'll have to figure out some way to signal the helicopter tomorrow."

"A helicopter! Oh, boy!"

"Yeah, oh boy," David repeated.

He laid the rifle on a narrow ledge and sat down on the ground, suddenly weary. "Gee, I haven't eaten yet!" he exclaimed.

Locating the knapsack, he unfastened the straps and felt inside. Beside the empty vacuum bottles there seemed to be a lot of wadded-up wax paper. He found one orange and one candy bar. "Did you eat all the sandwiches?" he asked sharply.

"No."

"What did you do with them?"

"They're in there."

David rummaged some more and finally came up with one lone package of two sandwiches. "How many sandwiches did you eat?" he demanded.

"I don't remember."

"Okay, then, how many were left over?"

"Two."

"Two packages, or two sandwiches?"

"Two sandwiches," Winston said in a small voice.

"You mean this is all that's left!" David yelped. "I told you to take it easy!"

"I was hungry. I hadn't had anything to eat since lunch yesterday."

"Well, you big pig!" David exploded. "You're apt not to get anything more for a couple of days!"

He unwrapped the last two sandwiches and bit into one of them. It was peanut butter and honey, a real energy sandwich, one of his favorites. Not exactly what he would choose for dog food, however.

"Wolf!"

"You're not going to feed 'em to the dog, are you?" Winston protested.

"Just one of them," David retorted. "And half that candy bar. You'd still be lost if it wasn't for Wolf."

They spent a miserable night. Although the wind could not find its way into their retreat, the cold seeped into their very bones. David warmed himself several times by doing calisthenics, but he got scant sleep. In the morning, as soon as the light was strong enough, he crawled out from under the big tree to see what could be done about attracting the attention of the rescue helicopter. When he came back some twenty minutes later, he found Winston crying.

"Hey, what's the matter?" he asked.

"I thought . . . you weren't . . . coming back!"

"What made you think that?"

"You . . ." Winston stared at his own feet, his mouth twisting. "You don't like me very much!"

David snorted. "You screw-ball! Even if I hated you, I wouldn't go off and leave you."

Briefly he explained what he had been doing. "There's a big snowbank on the other side of the ridge. You can help me break off evergreen boughs, and I'll lay them out in the shape of letters. We'll make a big sign for the plane pilot to see."

"My leg hurts so bad, I don't think I can help," Winston whimpered.

"I think you'd *better* help," David responded. "If you'd stir around a little, you wouldn't be so cold."

"I think my leg is broken."

"I thought you said you hurt your knee."

"Well, I think I broke my knee."

David sighed.

"Don't you even want to look at it?" Winston asked plaintively.

"I couldn't do anything for it if I did," David said. "The skin isn't broken, or you'd see blood seeping through your pants' leg. I expect it does hurt, but crying about it isn't going to make it feel any better. Are you coming with me?"

A wail of despair followed him out of the hideaway, but he did not turn back. On top of the ridge he had to brace himself to stand against the wind. Crouching in the lee of a boulder, he studied the country in the direction from which he had come the day before. In the gray light of dawn nothing looked familiar.

"Oh, boy!" he groaned.

He and Wolf could hike downhill and simply keep going until eventually they came to a road or a house, but that wouldn't solve any problems for Winston.

With a sigh, he got to his feet and strode down the slope to the timber below the big snowdrift. His original

thought had been to spell out the word HELP, but he
soon concluded that he would need an awful lot of evergreen boughs to make even one letter of any considerable
size. Nor was that the sum of his troubles. The sloping
surface of the big drift had thawed by day and frozen by
night until it had become a sheet of ice. Unless David
slammed his heels down and broke the crust with each
step, his feet would fly out from under him. Three times
he slid down the drift, and each time the wind sent his
branches whooshing after him. Wolf thought it was great
sport, but David did not share the big dog's delight.

Eventually he tramped a trail and stayed in it. He anchored the boughs by jabbing them straight down into the
drift, and he made only one letter—a big X. He didn't need
HELP or S.O.S., he realized, because the helicopter pilot
already knew that someone was lost.

He found Winston lying on his back with fir boughs
heaped over his legs and the rucksack pulled across his
chest. The sun's rays did not yet reach into the pocket at
the base of the ledge. "If you'd try to move around a little,
you wouldn't be so cold," he suggested, and realized he
was beginning to sound like a cracked phonograph record.

"I want my mother!" Winston sobbed.

"When the search planes see my X, it won't take 'em
long to get us out of here. Ever ridden in a helicopter,
Winston?"

"No."

David tried to speak cheerfully, but the youngster
needed warmth, not words. Finally David said, "Look,
Winston, you've got to move around. I've been working,
and I'm plenty warm. If you don't get going, you're going
to catch pneumonia."

"But I can't walk! You know I can't!" Winston wailed.

"So try something else!" David snapped. "You big baby! Look!"

Plumping down on his bottom with his legs out in front of him, arms braced a little behind him, David raised his right leg as if it were injured. "Now watch!"

By drawing up his "good" leg and using his arms as crutches, he was able to swing his whole body a step backward. He took a second step and a third. As a means of locomotion the effectiveness of the method surprised even him. "Nothing to it," he said. "Just go like an inchworm."

"I can't!"

"You haven't even tried! Now try something before I get disgusted and slug you!"

Winston looked at him in numb unbelief.

"Move!" David bellowed.

Winston began to cry, but he moved. The first time, he didn't quite master the rhythm, but with David glaring at him, he tried again. He took another hitch and another. Suddenly a faint smile flickered across his blue, frightened face. "Hey, I can do it!"

"Sure you can! Okay. See if you can make it to where you were yesterday. We'll at least be in the sun, and if a plane comes over I can run up to the ridge and try to attract attention."

The youngster nodded. With David carrying the rifle and rucksack and offering step-by-step encouragement, Winston rump-bumped himself all the way up to the hollow among the rocks. "Boy, it's lots warmer up here!" he exclaimed.

"You just got your blood to circulating, that's all," David told him.

They divided an orange, the last of their food, and they talked about their hopes for rescue. David picked up the .22 rifle. He knew it was not loaded because he had checked it the night before. "Do you have any shells for this thing?"

Winston shook his head. "I used the last one on Wolf."

A dozen feet away the big shepherd lay with his nose to the wind. At mention of his name he got up and came over. He stood, an amiable giant, too mannerly to mention that he had had no breakfast. "Too bad I didn't train you as a messenger dog," David observed.

All morning they waited and watched. David wondered if his mother would remember that Blitz was arriving by plane from California. Gee, it would be great to have Blitz again. Once they heard the distant drone of a small plane, and David ran to the crest of the ridge, but the craft passed far to the north. Toward noon Winston decided to hitch himself up to the top to look at David's X. David sat down beside him and offered to race, and presently they were both laughing.

When they reached the ridge and looked across the miles of wilderness, their attention was drawn immediately to a column of smoke rising from beyond a hill a mile or more away. "Hey, what's that?" Winston exclaimed, pointing.

"I don't know," David admitted. "I didn't see it an hour ago. I don't think it would be a forest fire starting this time of year, but that's an awful lot of smoke for a camp-fire."

"Maybe it's a signal fire," said Winston, his high voice rising higher with excitement.

"Let's watch it awhile and see what it does," David suggested.

They found a place out of the wind and sat side by side. The smoke continued to rise in a thin column from the same spot. "It's not spreading," David said finally. "Somebody must be controlling it."

Winston nodded. "It's gotta be a signal fire, David. It wouldn't smoke that much unless they wanted it to smoke, would it?"

"I think you're right," David conceded. "It must be a signal." He stood up. "What do you want to do? I could hike over there in forty minutes or so. Would you be willing to wait here?"

The corners of Winston's mouth began to twitch. "What if you didn't come back!"

"I'd come back. Look, if you don't want to stay alone, I can leave Wolf. He'll stay with you if I tell him. You'll be all right. I can be back with help in two or three hours at the very most."

"I don't want to stay here by myself!" came the familiar wail.

David regarded him thoughtfully. He couldn't much blame the youngster. "Okay," he decided aloud, "I'll carry you. We won't be able to go very fast, though, because I'll have to put you down when I get tired. And I'll have to walk back each time to get the rucksack and the .22."

"Can't I just put the rucksack on and hold onto the gun?"

"Oh, great! You'll carry the gun! What do you think I am—a pack horse? It's all I can do to lift you."

Before they started out, David made a special effort to memorize several geographic points on line with the smoke signal. That way he could stay on course even when he dropped down in a hollow and could no longer see the smoke. On the very first carry, he tried to cover too much ground and almost played himself out, but he quickly learned to pace himself. The fourth time he brought the knapsack and rifle up, he was delighted to find that in his absence Winston had made progress inchworm style. The boy was trying.

With painful slowness they crept closer to the column of smoke. The distance began to seem more like three miles than the one mile they had estimated. David ate snow to assuage his thirst, but he began to feel light-headed from hunger.

Finally, along in midafternoon, they topped the last hill and looked directly down on the signal fire. "Hey, there's a tent!" Winston exclaimed over David's shoulder.

"I've got to set you down again," David gasped.

The scene below was not what he had expected. He had hoped for a road and automobiles. Here was neither. The tent was an old-style wall tent with a stovepipe sticking out the top. The setup looked like a sheepherder's camp.

As he stood catching his breath, a man wearing khaki field clothes came out of the tent. He looked to the left and to the right and strode toward the smoldering campfire. He prodded it with a long stick, then, as if alarmed by some sound, shot a look over his shoulder.

David followed the direction of the man's gaze, but could see nothing out of the ordinary. "He sure acts nervous," Winston observed.

David nodded, his curiosity aroused. The fellow placed

some evergreen boughs on the fire and took another uneasy look around before going back inside the tent.

"I don't think they're looking for us," Winston said.

"I don't, either," David admitted. "If they were looking
for us, they'd be sitting up here on the hill with a pair of
field glasses."

"Who do you suppose they are?" Winston asked, lowering his voice almost to a whisper.

"I don't know. Let's find out." Drawing in a deep
breath, David shouted, "Hello! Anybody home?"

Instantly the man reappeared. He ran to look down the
draw below the tent, then whirled as though he expected
something to pop up behind him. David yelled again and
waved his arms. Finally the man looked up, and the boys
heard him say, presumably to someone inside the tent, "It
isn't Harry. It's a couple of kids up on the hill with a
dog."

Then to the boys the man shouted, "Look out for the
bear!"

"Where?" David called.

"Yeah!" said the man, evidently thinking David had repeated the word "bear."

David tried again. *"Where is the bear?"*

"I don't know!" came the answer.

David turned to Winston. "They must have had a run-in
with a bear. I'll bet that smoke is a signal for help."

"Gee, I hope they're not out of food," the boy responded.

David knelt. "Better climb aboard again. If there's a
bear around, we'll be safer down there."

"What about the .22 and your knapsack?"

"I'll have to go back for them later. I don't suppose

there's any real danger, but I'd just as soon not leave you sitting."

"If there's no danger," Winston said, hitching into position, "why is that man so scared?"

David lurched to his feet. "Maybe he's a dude. Maybe he doesn't know that wild bears will run from you. Unless you corner them, of course, or get between a mother and her cubs—something like that."

"Maybe it's a grizzly bear."

"Well, keep your eyes open," David advised. "If you see a grizzly, you're liable to think you're riding in the Kentucky Derby. I don't argue with those babies!"

"One of them's carrying the other," the man below said, apparently unaware that his voice carried plainly to the boys.

"They haven't even heard about us," said Winston.

Dense timber blanketed the far slope of the draw. The tent was pitched beside a small stream that meandered through a meadow of winter-flattened swale grass. David descended the treeless slope and strode across the flat. The man at the tent came toward them, but kept looking back over his shoulder.

"Hi!" David called, wading into the shallow creek.

"Hello, there!"

Up close, the fellow reminded David of Murray Williams. Tall and well-built, a little on the heavy side, he was probably around forty years old. His worn field boots indicated that he was no stranger to the back country.

"You're packing quite a load, fella."

"Yeah, Winston hurt his . . ." David began.

"Winston! You're not the kid they've been talking about on the radio!"

"Have you got any food, mister?" Winston piped. "We're awfully hungry."

"Food? You bet!" The stranger looked at David and at Wolf. "You must be that other kid that's missing. Is that the tracking dog?"

"That's him," David said proudly. He walked the final twenty feet into the camp and dropped to one knee to unload his human burden. "We thought your smoke signal was for us. I guess, though, you've got problems of your own, huh?"

"You better believe it! A bear came into camp just about breakfast time this morning. He scared off our horses and attacked Ward Brownell, the fellow I'm working with. I'm Jim McGivotte, by the way. We're doing a survey for a mining company."

David stepped forward to shake hands. "David Hollis."

"Ward's in the tent," McGivotte continued. "He's pretty well chewed up. I don't know what's got into that bear."

"Maybe he just came out of hibernation," David suggested.

"I don't know." McGivotte glanced over his shoulder. "Usually they aren't on the fight when they first come out. If anything, they're extra shy. But it took all three of us yelling and pounding to drive him off. Harry—he's the fellow who wrangles our horses and cooks for us—went for help about eight o'clock this morning. I started this smudge in hopes of attracting the attention of the helicopter that's looking for you kids over on Homestead Creek."

"Was it a grizzly bear?" Winston asked.

"No, just a black bear. Kind of a small one, at that. Not more than a two-year-old."

"Do you really think he'll come back?" David started to
say, but he interrupted himself. "Look at Wolf; he smells
him!"

The young dog stood stiff-legged, the hair erect along
his spine from ears to tail. A growl rumbled deep in his
chest.

"I'm glad you have that guy with you," said McGivotte.
"The only gun we have is out of commission. Harry had a
.22 automatic rifle he was shooting chucks with this morning, but he left it leaning against a log, and one of the
horses stepped on it when the bear came."

"It probably won't be back," David said, "do you
think?"

McGivotte snorted. "He's already been back twice—
once right after Harry left and again about forty minutes
ago. We've banged pans together and scared him off, but
I'm afraid he'll get braver when night comes."

"We got a .22 back over the hill," Winston said.

"Yeah, I can go get it," David volunteered.

The surveyor shook his head. "Too dangerous. I
wouldn't want you to go alone, and I can't leave Ward."
He groaned. "I wish Harry would get back. It scares me to
think he might have run into trouble."

"Maybe he looked for the horses before he went for
help," David said.

Behind him, Winston uttered a sharp, clearly audible
gasp. Even as David turned the boy shrilled, "There he is!
There he is! There's the bear!"

12.

Rogue Bear

The bear had ambled out of the timber some sixty yards up the draw from the surveyors' camp. When Winston yelled, Wolf turned and caught sight of the intruder. Instantly, he roared in challenge.

"Better grab your dog!" Jim McGivotte snapped.

The admonition came a second too late. While David stood looking at the bear, surprised by its patchy appearance, Wolf dashed past him. "Wolf! Wolf, no!" he screamed. "Wolf, come!"

The big dog kept right on going. Either he couldn't hear over the thunder of his own barking or he simply chose to ignore the frantic command. In David's mind flashed a picture of a limp shepherd, neck broken by a single swipe of a powerful forearm, and he started forward on the run.

"Come back, kid! Come back!" shouted McGivotte.

The bear emitted an explosive woof of surprise and rose up on his hind legs as the dog rushed toward him. He lashed out with a lethal forepaw, but at the last instant Wolf swerved. Well out of reach, the dog circled, feinting, all the while disclaiming at the top of his voice the black invader's right to occupy any part of the territory.

David came to a halt. He seemed always to underestimate Wolf. Rowdy and rambunctious though he was, the big dog had never lacked for brains. Instinct, if nothing else, had warned him that the bear was dangerous.

Behind David, camp cookware clattered and banged. "They don't like noise," he heard McGivotte shout. "Make all the racket you can!"

The injured man inside the tent was already banging away. Winston and McGivotte joined in, and Winston's shrill voice rose above the clamor. "Yowie! Go away, bear! Go away!"

Spurred on by the commotion in camp, Wolf nipped the bear on the rump. The snarling beast dropped to all fours and whirled to swat murderously at his elusive adversary. David scooped up a club. "Go on, get out of here!" he bellowed.

Apparently the bear had not bargained on a reception this energetically hostile. With a squall of annoyance, he retreated at a shambling run. Wolf not only escorted him, but snatched a mouthful of hair as the bruin sprang up the trunk of a lodgepole pine tree and scrambled to safety.

"Wolf, you big sap," David shouted. "Come here! Wolf, come!"

Like an overgrown yo-yo, the excited dog jumped again and again at the tree in an effort to reach his quarry. Only when he saw the stick in David's hand and concluded that the boy meant to use it on him, did he heed the command to come. Then gaily, without a twinge of conscience, his tail held high, jaws gaping in a grin of enormous satisfaction, he came galloping back.

"You chowder-head!" David exclaimed, slapping the dog in rough affection. "If you crowd that guy, he'll make hamburger of you."

"He was lucky and so were you," Jim McGivotte said, striding up to join them. "Let's get back to camp. That's no ordinary black bear. That's a rogue!"

A tremor in the man's voice caused David to glance up sharply. All color had left McGivotte's face. The fellow was afraid!

Feeling oddly adult, David said, "He probably won't bother us again, Mr. McGivotte, now that he knows Wolf is here."

The surveyor snorted. "We surprised him a little, that's all. He isn't scared. When he comes down out of that tree, look out!"

David thought then of Winston's .22 and mentioned it. "I could go get it and be back in twenty minutes," he said.

McGivotte shook his head. "It's not worth the risk. A .22 isn't much of a weapon against a bear, anyway."

"It would be better than nothing," David argued. "At close range it would do the job."

Again McGivotte shook his head. "We'd better all stick together."

David decided not to press the subject. As he walked back toward the tent, he gathered an armload of firewood. He didn't mean to show off. He actually thought the surveyor was making a big to-do over nothing. When he had helped Link build fence on the Ittlesby ranch, they had seen any number of bears. They'd never been concerned about them and never had any trouble, either.

In a few minutes the bear backed down out of the tree and ambled away in the direction from which he had come. David waited a little while, then said casually, "Now might be a good time to go get that .22."

"I *would* feel a lot safer if we had some kind of weapon," McGivotte confessed, "but if something happened, I'd . . ."

"Don't worry about me. I'll have Wolf along. That bear's not a bit anxious to collect any more tooth marks on his hide."

Belatedly, the notion occurred to David that this frightened adult was concerned not for him but for the safety of the camp while the dog was absent. "Couldn't you build up your fire," he suggested, "so as to have some blazing sticks to throw? Wild animals don't like fire."

"How far away is that gun?"

"Just a couple of hundred yards over the top of the hill. The bear couldn't possibly sneak up on me. You'd see him if he started up that bare hillside, and you could yell to me."

With reluctance the surveyor gave his consent. "You'd better take along some shells for the gun. But for Pete's sake," he begged, "don't take any chances!"

Even though David felt sure the danger was vastly overrated, his heart was pounding with nervous excitement by the time he had crossed the bottom of the draw. He turned to look before he started up the hill, but did not see the bear. Then he smiled at his own apprehension.

"Didn't know you were working for a sissy, did you, Wolf?" he said to the big dog beside him.

He looked back several times more, but caught no glimpse of the wandering marauder. He found the rifle and his rucksack just as he had left them and made the return trip without incident. In his absence Jim McGivotte had prepared supper. David watched Wolf inhale a gallon of assorted groceries and suddenly realized that he, too, was famished.

"The helicopter wrecked," Winston greeted him. "Mr.

Brownell has a transistor radio. They told about it on the five o'clock news."

"That's right," McGivotte affirmed. "The copter crashed on take-off early this morning. That's probably why they haven't found us. No one seriously hurt, I guess."

Inside the tent David met Ward Brownell. The condition of the injured surveyor shocked him. Brownell lay on an air mattress in his sleeping bag, his eyes bright with fever. He would speak rationally one moment, and then his mind would twist with delirium. At those times he seemed to be a Marine officer wounded and waiting for evacuation to a field hospital behind the lines.

"How badly is he hurt?" David asked later, when he and McGivotte were gathering firewood.

"He has bad bites on his leg, and I would suspect broken ribs. His left arm is pretty badly shredded, too. All we had was some disinfectant and some aspirin. We got the bleeding stopped, but the pain must be awful."

"I don't think that I'd have been so brave about going after the .22 if I'd seen Mr. Brownell first," David admitted.

"I'm scared to death something has happened to Harry," the surveyor responded. "He should have been back with help hours ago."

They piled up fuel to last through the night and tried to devise plans for defense. McGivotte wanted Winston to attempt to climb into the sturdy branches of a fir tree so that he would be out of the way if the bear came back, but the boy refused. He seemed to fear that somehow he might be left all by himself.

Survey equipment stacked neatly in a makeshift pup tent attracted David's attention. "What are these?" he asked, pointing to the six red-and-white spear-like objects.

"Range poles. We use them to sight on when we're establishing a line."

David's understanding of what surveyors did was extremely limited, but the range poles interested him. Made of three-quarter-inch tubular aluminum, they looked to be about six feet long. One end was solid metal with a blunt point that could be stuck into the ground. "May I look at one?" he asked.

"Sure. Think you might take up surveying?"

Experimentally, David hefted one of the red-and-white markers. It was lightweight and balanced nicely in his hand. "If this point was sharpened, this would make a dandy javelin," he said.

"Javelin? Hey!" McGivotte exclaimed. "I never thought about that. You mean, to use on the bear."

David nodded. "With a .22 you won't dare shoot until he's real close. If you shouldn't happen to kill him, we might need something like this pretty bad."

Winston's eyes widened at the talk of hand-to-hand combat. "Do you really think I should climb into the tree?" he said.

"I think you'd be awfully smart to climb into the tree," David assured him.

"You could be our lookout," McGivotte added.

The latter idea appealed to the youngster. With David's help, he managed to pull himself into the lower branches of a giant fir a few yards from the campfire. "How high should I go?" he asked.

"If you're fairly high," said McGivotte, "the bear won't even know you're up there. Try to pick a comfortable place to sit because you may have to stay for a while."

"What do you think? Should I try to sharpen one of these range poles for a spear?" David inquired.

McGivotte nodded. "Go ahead. Maybe you can file it against a rock."

"Hey," Winston called from his evergreen refuge, "that bear can climb trees."

"Sure. All black bears can," David said.

"Well, then, this isn't such a safe place!"

"If you can think of a better one, let me know," David retorted.

Three-quarters of an hour later dusk was stealing up the draw when Wolf jumped to his feet and growled. David hurried to get hold of his dog, and Jim McGivotte snatched up the .22. "There he is!" Winston shouted. "I can see him. He's coming this way!"

As the bruin shambled into view among the trees above camp, Wolf lunged and nearly jerked David off his feet. The ridges reverberated with the big mongrel's barking.

"I wouldn't let him loose," McGivotte warned. "If I have to shoot, I don't want to risk hitting him."

"I'll tie him up," David said. "Toss me that rope, would you?"

From the tent a querulous voice called, "Who is it? Has B Company been heard from? Sergeant!"

"No help there," McGivotte said tensely.

David secured Wolf to Winston's tree, but made certain the knots he tied could be released in a hurry. He picked up the range pole he had just finished sharpening, then set it down again in favor of a couple of empty pans. If the bear could be frightened away, he would rather Mc-Givotte didn't try to kill it. A wounded bear could be a truly fearsome thing.

Looking bigger than he had seemed by broad daylight, the interloper approached to within twenty yards. He paid no attention to the racket of the dog. When McGivotte lobbed a flaming stick at him, he dodged but even then did not retreat. Instead he wandered over to the surveyors' food cache slung from a pole lashed horizontally between two trees. Unable to reach the tarpaulin-wrapped bundle from the ground, he climbed one of the trees.

"Do you suppose," David suggested, "he would go away if we fed him?"

McGivotte shrugged. "I hate to encourage him. He may be hungry, all right, but I'm sure that's only a part of the problem. I tell you, he doesn't act like a normal bear!"

Overhead Winston began chattering about something. When David could silence Wolf for a few seconds, the boy announced excitedly, "I heard another dog barking. When Wolf was barking, another dog barked. Someone's coming!"

"Probably an echo," McGivotte said. "Do you hear it now?"

"No, it's not barking now. But it wasn't an echo. I really heard it."

"Maybe your friend who went for help is coming," said David.

"It sounded like it came from where we came from," Winston called.

"Couldn't have," McGivotte asserted.

"Why don't we yell and see if anybody answers," David suggested.

"I will!" Winston volunteered. Not waiting for permission, he bellowed, "HEL–L–L——P!"

Even Wolf fell silent. In the sudden quiet, small sounds came alive—twigs popping as they burned, fir boughs softly rustling in a vagrant breeze, the voices of the creek babbling merrily, the bear moving in the tree. David listened, but he heard no barking in the distance.

"The sound of a dog carries a long way," he said finally. "How far are we from the nearest ranch house?"

"It didn't come from a ranch. It came from up on the mountain," Winston declared.

McGivotte shook his head. "We're a long way from anywhere. If he actually heard a dog, it must be Harry coming with a rescue party. Though I don't know why he'd bring a dog."

"I heard one," Winston insisted.

Inside the tent, Ward Brownell's voice rose in delirium. "Sergeant! Sergeant! Corporal Huff!"

"Maybe I'd better check on him," McGivotte said.

The bear stayed in the tree for ten minutes or more. He made considerable noise breaking twigs and branches, but he didn't discover a way to reach the food. When he came down, he boldly looked over the camp. David picked up a rock the size of an apricot and threw it. "Git outa here! Go on! Beat it!"

The missile caught the bear in the ribs and made him jump. His squall of anger rose above Wolf's fierce baying. Ambling to another tree, the young bruin reared up on his hind legs and with his powerful foreclaws raked the bark as high up as he could reach.

"That other dog's barking again!" Winston shouted.

David couldn't hear over Wolf's carrying-on. "Hush up, you!" he ordered.

As the big dog reluctantly subsided, David stood very

still. He was about to conclude that Winston was imagining things when Wolf began to rumble again, and suddenly off in the gathering dusk there was a dog barking! "Hey, I hear him!" he cried. "He's not too far away, either!"

McGivotte frowned. "It does sound as if it's coming from over the hill, doesn't it? That can't be Harry."

"Maybe it's the sheriff," Winston called. "Maybe he followed David."

"How? That's not a bloodhound's yodeling." The surveyor regarded David in bafflement. "Does anyone else in Winnegar have a dog that's trained like Wolf?"

"Not that I know of."

"Swell," said McGivotte. "It's probably a couple of Boy Scouts with their cocker spaniel!"

The bear didn't leave. As the darkness deepened, he became invisible among the trees except when the firelight touched his eyes, and then two ruby reflectors would flash eerily and disappear. Every time a twig snapped, Wolf barked and Jim McGivotte jumped. David wondered privately whether the surveyor would be able to shoot accurately if the need arose. Uneasily he built up the fire.

All at once, from out of the night, came a voice that rolled like thunder. "WHAT'S GOING ON DOWN THERE!"

Wolf spun around as if he had been stung. Whimpers of joy erupted in his throat as he lunged to the end of his tether. Furiously his great bushy tail whipped the air.

"It's Murray Williams, Wolf's owner," David cried. Cupping his hands about his mouth, he shouted, "WE GOT BEAR TROUBLE! BE CAREFUL!"

"HELP!" Winston screeched.

Lights flickered on the ridge. David counted at least four. "I don't know how they managed to find us," he said, "but I'm sure glad they're here!"

"I hope they've got a gun bigger than this peashooter I'm holding," McGivotte said.

They stood with their backs to the fire and watched the points of light slowly descend the hill. David became aware of a tearing sound somewhere behind him, but Wolf was making such a racket that its significance didn't strike him for several seconds. When finally he did wake up and swivel in alarm, he saw the tent shudder. Almost simultaneously, Winston's shrill voice rose in warning, "Stop him! He's trying to get in the back of the tent!"

Sheer horror distorted the features of Jim McGivotte. "We've got to get Ward out of there!" he exclaimed. However, he didn't move. He stood and jerked this way and that as if he didn't know whether to put the .22 down or take it with him.

David stepped to Wolf and yanked the knot that would set the dog free. Then he ran to the tent and McGivotte ran with him. As they drew back the flaps at the entrance, a black bulk thrust through a ragged vertical slash in the back wall. By the light of a gas lantern swaying from the ridge pole, David could see the glistening wetness of tongue and fangs—the bear was that close. As the beast's snarling filled the tent, David and McGivotte both shouted. Bending as one, they got hold of the tarpaulin under Ward Brownell and yanked him out of the tent— bed, air mattress, and all. David kept right on tugging to put distance between the injured man and the bear. McGivotte let go to grab up the .22 again.

Wolf meanwhile had run around the tent. Sounds of battle erupted inside. The lantern jumped, casting crazy patterns of light and shadow on the canvas walls. Canned goods, dishes, and cookware clattered and crashed to the ground. Glass tinkled, and suddenly the whole tent brightened as fire flared around the lantern.

Leaving Brownell, David snatched up his range-pole spear. "Don't try to go in there!" McGivotte yelled.

Another loud crash accented the snarling of the combatants. The bear emitted a bleat of pain, and an instant later the stove tumbled out the front flap, spewing sparks and red embers. Right behind the stove scooted Wolf, his ears back, tail tucked. By then flames from the lantern were leaping along the top of the ridge pole. As the bear burst out the side of the tent, David ran for cover. Guy ropes popped and tent stakes flew.

"Shoot! Shoot!" Winston yelled from his perch.

"No, don't!" David shouted. "He's had enough. Give him a chance to run!"

The words had barely passed his lips when he heard the brittle pop of the gun. He saw the bear swing his head to bite at his shoulder as if he'd been stung by a bee. Instantly Wolf darted in to slash at the unprotected flank. The bear squalled in anger and turned to swat at the dog. Missing, he caught sight of Jim McGivotte. He charged so suddenly the surveyor had no chance to dodge. The .22 discharged into the air as the man went down under the impact of two hundred pounds of snarling fury.

In deadly embrace, surveyor and bear rolled together. David ran with his range pole to join the fray, but couldn't drive the spear home for fear of hitting McGivotte or Wolf. Desperately he poked and prodded, and suddenly the angry bruin turned on him. He whirled to run and tripped over a log. Sprawling on his hands and knees, he scrabbled frantically to get out of reach. Claws raked his leg. He yelped and heard a curious answering cry of concern that could only have come from a canine throat.

Wolf seemed to be everywhere. He snapped in the bear's face. He slashed its rump. He worried its flank. He dared the death-dealing forepaws. He swarmed over his wrathful opponent as if he were half a dozen dogs. David found himself trampled and buffeted but scarcely involved in the battle.

Like a tornado, the action rolled on across the camp site. When David scrambled to his feet, Jim McGivotte stood poised with the camp ax held in readiness. David bent swiftly to pick up his spear again, and stiffened in surprise. There were two dogs fighting the bear!

Blitz!

Unspoken, the name flashed across his mind. Incredibly, the second dog was Blitz. It just couldn't be, but it was! How had she gotten here? Who. . . ? A terrifying thought jolted him into motion. One blow, one glancing blow with those wicked claws, could end forever a promising show career, could easily snuff out a life.

"Hold it, David!" called Murray Williams. "Stand tight!"

He saw the deputy then, the light of the campfire full on his face, a big magnum revolver in his hand. "Don't shoot! You might hit one of the dogs!" David cried.

Taut with anxiety, he watched the two shepherds. They worked as a team. Blitz feinted a frontal assault, deliberately drawing the bear's attention to herself so that

Wolf might dart in to slash the unprotected rear. The beleaguered bruin roared in fury and stood up on his hind legs. Precisely then, the gun in Murray Williams' hand spoke, the report reverberating across the draw. The bear staggered, driven backward by the force of the impact, and without a sound crumpled to the earth.

Still trying to fathom the presence of Blitz, David watched the two dogs walk stiff-legged and rumbling around their fallen foe.

"Believe that stopped him," said Williams.

"But what's Blitz doing here?" David asked in bewilderment.

She heard her name and whirled. Whimpering and ecstatic, she came and launched herself at him. Wriggling like a great overgrown puppy, she climbed into his arms and sloshed his face with a sloppy tongue. Joyfully he thumped her lean ribs, and then she broke away to turn wild cartwheels of delight.

The bear was dead. Murray Williams held his big revolver in readiness, but the black mound remained inert when he pushed it with his toe.

Jim McGivotte walked forward slowly, still carrying the ax. "He isn't very big, but he sure played rough."

"Are you all right?" Williams asked.

The surveyor's quilted jacket hung in strings. He had blood on his face. "I'm all right. It's just a good thing that David was here to pull him off of me."

"How are you feeling, David?" the deputy asked. "Looked to me as though you sort of got run over."

David had to stop to think how he was. "I'm okay, I guess. I feel kind of shaky, is all."

He was amazed, actually. The leg the bear had clawed

stung a little, but it didn't hurt as badly as the shin bone he had rapped on the log when he fell. "What about Mr. Brownell?" he asked. "We moved him out of the tent in an awful hurry."

Flashlight beams darted and voices sounded as shadowy human shapes splashed across the creek. Overhead, snapping twigs marked Winston's descent from his perch in the tree. David turned to see three men moving into the light from the fire. He could not mistake the figure in the lead. Johnny's spare frame loomed a full head taller than either of his companions. David knew the next man, too. "Hey," he called in sudden delight. "It's my dad!"

"It's my dad, too!" Winston echoed. "Help me, someone!"

David hardly knew what to say. His father was the last person in the world he expected to see in a wilderness camp. Marshall Hollis never had had time to go hunting or hiking with his sons. Yet here he was.

"Are you all right, son?"

"How'd you get here?" David demanded foolishly.

His dad grinned. "I walked."

"Blitz brought us," Johnny said enthusiastically. "I could hardly hold her the last couple of miles."

"Blitz?"

Dad nodded. "When you didn't show up last night, Johnny insisted that you and Wolf were following Winston's trail. He . . ."

"I knew Blitz would track you if we could get her started in the right place," Johnny interrupted. "Winston's uncle remembered he'd borrowed some matches from you. That's where we started."

"Actually it wasn't quite that easy," Marshall Hollis remonstrated. "Murray Williams did the tracking until we got to your big X on the snowdrift. He followed the wounded deer. Then your scent must have been fresher because Blitz seemed to catch on fire."

David knelt to rough the excited shepherd. "When did you guys start?"

"We picked up Blitz at the airport at eleven-fifteen this morning," Dad replied. "We didn't stop at home. It must have been about two o'clock when we reached Homestead Creek."

"The sheriff thought we were a bunch of kooks," Johnny recalled gleefully.

"Yes," Dad agreed, "I think in the beginning Murray came along just to keep us from getting lost."

As he spoke, a branch gave way and Winston fell out of the tree. The boy tumbled only two or three feet, but when his father tried to catch him both went down. David was disgusted to hear the youngster begin to cry. Then he realized that Winston was laughing, not crying. Mr. Grosser began to laugh too, and both father and son sounded a little hysterical.

Above the merriment, a metallic clanging sounded faintly in the quiet night air. "Listen!" Johnny hissed.

The group fell silent. Off in the distance, a bell jangled rhythmically. "That's our wrangler, Harry!" exclaimed Jim McGivotte. "That's the bell on his lead mule."

For several minutes the trail music grew louder; then it abruptly ceased. From the darkness down the draw a man called out questioningly, "Jim?"

"The bear's dead, Harry. Come on in!"

The bell resumed its clanging, and presently four men on snorting, skitterish horses rode into camp. All four carried rifles in saddle scabbards. The lead rider had two pack animals in tow.

"You're too late for the fun," McGivotte greeted them. "What happened, Harry?"

The young fellow with the mules removed his cowboy hat and scratched the back of his head. "That ol' bear kept me up a tree for over four hours. I thought he never would leave."

Someone built up the fire, and as the newcomers dismounted, David recognized a man who had come unhesitatingly in another emergency. Dr. Hanson surveyed the wrecked tent and its scattered contents and remarked offhandedly, "Looks as if you've had some excitement."

While the doctor and some of the others took care of Ward Brownell, Harry turned a flashlight on the sprawling carcass of the bear. David was the one who spotted the hole where Murray Williams' shot had penetrated the skull just below and a little forward of one ear.

"Nice shooting," said the wrangler. "Well, look at this!"

The probing beam of the light had found a wound in the bear's flank, an old injury that had evidently abscessed and been draining for some time. David could see something that looked like a twig protruding from the sore. Harry touched it with a gloved hand. "That's an arrow broken off in there. Someone gut-shot him. No wonder he was on the prod. Poor devil!"

13.

Dog Show

"Afghan hounds number ten and number fourteen, please report to ring one . . . Exhibitors of German shepherd dogs, please pick up your arm bands at ring three."

A flurry of barking punctuated the announcement over the public address system. David glanced up and saw that a spectator to the annual dog show of the Gallatin Dog Club in Bozeman, Montana, had paused to look at two Doberman pinschers in a small exercise pen. He stroked Blitz. "If you made that kind of racket every time a stranger walked by," he told the glistening shepherd, "I'd strangle you."

Actually, here in the field house of Montana State University, a dozen dogs barking, or a hundred, didn't make much difference. Sound got lost in the vastness of the great domed stadium.

David laid aside the brush he had been using and picked up a big, heavy-fibered grooming mitt. In the three months since the encounter with the bear, he had spent countless hours bringing the shepherd's coat to luxuriant perfection. He had her standing now on the bottom row of a tier of unoccupied bleacher seats. A few feet from him a woman was using a dog crate as a grooming table for her toy poodle. Van-type trucks and station wagons belonging to professional handlers, grooming setups, exercise pens, and trash barrels took up most of the floor space on this end of the building.

Johnny appeared, his footsteps noiseless on the hard-packed dirt floor of the field house. "Hey, David, the Etonhill station wagon just pulled in. They had car trouble in Idaho."

David looked in the direction of the vehicle entrance, but his view was blocked. "I'm glad they made it. I'm real anxious to see what Blitz will do against her own brother and Princess Tanya."

Two days ago, in the first show of the annual Montana Copper Circuit, Blitz had won Best of Breed when she defeated two champions. However, the Etonhill dogs, busy competing in West Coast shows, had not been present.

German shepherd dogs were being paged again over the public address system when David's father came striding into the grooming area. "Hurry up, Son, you're supposed to be at ring three right now."

David tossed a knowing grin at Johnny. This was the first dog show Marshall Hollis had ever attended. "I've already got my number, Dad," he said, turning to display the paper band on his left arm. "There's no rush. They're not through with the boxers yet."

He laid aside the mitt and set Blitz up, posing her in the traditional show stance of the German shepherd. She stood as if cast of bronze—head alert, top line sloping smoothly from shoulders to tail, left hind leg well back, right hind leg forward under the body. "How does she look?"

A man and woman strolling past paused to admire the striking young shepherd. "Isn't he beautiful!" exclaimed the woman.

"She looks great," Johnny said. "Heinie would sure be proud if he could see her now."

Dad had a copper-colored show catalogue in his hands. "I don't find Blitz in here," he said, scowling at the listing of German shepherd dogs.

David looked over his shoulder and pointed. "Here, Dad. Etonhill Country Lady. That's Blitz."

"Etonhill Country Lady! Why didn't they use her right name?"

"That's her registered name. Blitz is just her call name."

Johnny pointed to another entry. "Here's Etonhill Country Squire. That's Blitz' brother."

Spectators at ring three applauded as the Best of Breed in boxers was chosen. "Let's go see how Squire makes out," David said.

Mom and Harvey were saving seats for them among the folding chairs at ringside. "Where's Shad?" Mom greeted Johnny.

"Over on the other side with my folks. They're keeping him out of the dirt."

While the winning boxer was being photographed in the ring with the judge, handlers with their German shepherds gathered at the gate. "Shouldn't you be over there?" Dad said to David.

"No, they'll judge all the dogs—the males, that is—first."

There were seven male German shepherd dogs listed in the catalogue. The lone entry in the Puppy class was awarded a blue ribbon. Then two Novice dogs were judged, and they were followed by a single Bred-by-Exhibitor dog.

"Well, I don't see much to this," Marshall Hollis said. "Where does the obedience come in?"

David blinked in astonishment. "This isn't obedience, Dad. This is the breed ring. The dogs are being judged on looks and character—stuff like that."

"Oh. Well, why don't they just put them all in the ring together, then, and pick out the best one?"

"It's not quite that simple," David said. "You see, they have to get a winner in each class, and then they put all the winners together, and the judge picks out what's called the Winners Dog."

"Seems as if he could do that without all this fussing."

David caught himself frowning as he tried to explain. "The thing is, Dad, this is just a small show. In a big show, there might be as many as ten or fifteen dogs in each class. A judge couldn't have fifty or sixty dogs in the ring all at once; so he has to do it this way. If you follow your catalogue and watch, you'll see how it sort of builds up. The dog that eventually wins Best of Breed will have beaten every other dog in the breed."

"Look, David!" Mom interrupted. "There's a dog that looks just like Blitz!"

He turned at a tug on his arm and saw Price Sargent hurrying toward ring three. He had met the professional handler in person just three weeks ago when he had flown to California, at Walter Eton's expense, to have Blitz bred. The shepherd at the handler's side did indeed look very much like Blitz.

"That's Etonhill Country Squire. That's Blitz' brother, Mom."

"And is that Price Sargent?"

The man who was one of the nation's top dog handlers

wore a rumpled business suit. He was of medium height and sturdily built with graying hair. His pleasantly rugged face was entirely undistinguished.

"His eyes always look kind of sleepy," David said in half-apology, "but he doesn't miss a thing."

While a steward put an arm band on him, Price Sargent glanced with deceptive casualness at the other German shepherds awaiting their turn in the ring. His gaze fell on Blitz, and he looked up swiftly. His slight nod of recognition gave David a tremendous feeling of importance.

Country Squire easily won the blue ribbon in the class for Open dogs. Then he remained in the ring as the first-place dogs from the other classes returned to compete for Winners Dog. Again the Etonhill entry was waved to first place.

David told Blitz to stay and strode to meet Price Sargent as he came out of the ring. "Squire is sure looking good, Mr. Sargent."

"Yeah, he's coming along. How are you, kid? They tell me Blitz went Best of Breed at Billings."

"Yes, sir. I thought she might even win the Group, but she was beaten by a boxer."

Sargent smiled. "A Group second is not bad for a beginner. Did you see Walt yet?"

"Mr. Eton? Is he here?"

"Expected to be." The handler scanned the spectator areas. Several hundred people seemed a scant handful among the vast tiers of seats. "I don't just lay my eyes on him, but I imagine he's here."

"Gee, I hope Blitz does good today," David said.

Price Sargent glanced toward Blitz, who was sitting beside Johnny. She watched David's every move with alert expectancy. "And I wouldn't worry too much," he said.

While the single Bred-by-Exhibitor bitch and the two American-Breds were being judged, David gave Blitz a final smoothing with his hands. There were eight entries in Open. Blitz faced stiff competition. As the class was called, he looked once more to make sure he had his breed-ring number on his arm and not his obedience number.

The judge, a slight, elderly man in a gray suit, checked his book to be certain the class was all present, then made a sweeping motion to the left with his arm. "Take 'em around," he said.

The woman who chanced to be in the lead broke into a run. She had to run in order to move her entry at a fast trot, the gait at which German shepherds best display their fitness as working dogs. The other handlers followed single file. Nobody had to tell them not to crowd up on one another. Beside the importance of sportsmanship and manners, each one wanted the judge to have a clear, un-obstructed view of his own dog.

The judge stood in the middle of the big rectangular ring while handlers and dogs made three complete cir-cuits. Then he signaled for a halt and indicated with a motion of both hands for the class to line up facing him. Panting from excitement as well as exertion, David stacked Blitz just as he had posed her earlier for his dad and Johnny.

"Always watch the judge," Price Sargent had warned him. "Position your dog as quickly as possible and then stand out of the way. When the judge looks in your direc-tion, he wants to see your dog, not a view of your rear side."

Slowly the judge moved along the line. To make their

dogs look alert, some of the handlers carried tidbits or squeaker toys. David waited until the little gray man stood before Blitz, then said softly, "Where's Muggins!"

Instantly Blitz stiffened to attention. Harvey's dog was her favorite playmate. Without moving any of her feet, she conveyed an impression of eagerness and vitality. David was well-pleased, but if the judge was impressed he gave no sign.

Now the handlers were called upon to gait their dogs one at a time. The judge told the woman in the lead exactly what he wanted. She took her dog at a trot directly away from him, turned left along the far side of the ring, then came back on the diagonal straight to him. The triangle pattern not only gave him a side view of the dog in action, but views going and coming. When the woman returned, she very quickly posed her dog, and the judge went over it carefully with his hands.

One by one, each dog was gaited and set up. David tried to remember everything Price Sargent had told him. He thought Blitz showed well, but the little judge didn't change expression from one dog to the next. When he had seen each of them, he walked down the line of dogs, viewing and comparing them from the front and then from the rear. Once more a wave of the arm sent the whole class around the ring. Three times they made the circle, and then the judge held up his hand to halt them. He pointed to David. "Blue."

Along one side of the ring, near the judge's table, were the place markers, four wooden signs on individual standards bearing big painted numerals. David moved to stand in front of number one. In delight he thumped his dog.

The judge handed ribbons to the four who had placed.

David thanked him and stuffed his award into a pocket as the winners of the other classes for German shepherd dog bitches re-entered the ring. Five minutes later he moved again to the first-place marker to receive the purple Winners ribbon.

Now Blitz must meet the Winners Dog and three Specials, including Etonhill Princess Tanya, who were champions already, for selection of Best of Breed. David supposed Price Sargent would handle Tanya and let his assistant handle Squire, because Tanya needed only two Best in Show awards to tie the all-time record for show-winning German shepherds. He was surprised, therefore, when the handler came into the ring with Squire. "Dog number eighteen is absent," he heard Sargent tell the steward.

He didn't intend to exhibit Tanya!

Before David had time to figure out the reason for the handler's decision, the judge waved the class into motion. Step by step, the pattern of the previous classes was repeated. Although the little judge had gone over both Squire and Blitz, he checked each again just as carefully as he examined the two remaining Specials. He gaited the class as a group and individually. He studied them front and rear, and finally his finger pointed to Blitz.

Johnny was at the gate as David floated out of the ring carrying a fistful of ribbons and a gleaming copper trophy. "Wahoo, boy! You beat out Etonhill with one of their own dogs!"

Dad stood up beaming. "Was that Etonhill Princess Tanya that Price Sargent was showing? Haven't you told me she's the best German shepherd in the country?"

"No, Dad. That wasn't Tanya. It was Squire again. I don't know why he didn't show Tanya."

"Two reasons," said a voice behind him.

David turned. "Oh, hi, Mr. Sargent! Mom, Dad, this is Price Sargent. And this is my brother, Harvey, and Johnny Martz, whom I told you about."

The handler shook hands with Marshall Hollis, nodded to Mom and Harvey and shook hands with Johnny. "The kid here is quite a handler," he said to Dad.

"How come you didn't enter Tanya?" David asked.

"Like I said, two reasons. I think Blitz is good enough to win the Group, and that's worth major points today. The other reason is that I didn't want to get Tanya beaten. She's been off her feed for a couple of days, and, frankly"—the handler smiled "—I'm not sure she could win over Blitz anyhow."

"Is Blitz really that good?" Dad asked.

"Well, I wouldn't say she hasn't any faults—I've never seen a perfect dog yet," Sargent said, "but she'll do until something better comes along."

As they stood talking, another man joined the group. He was sixtyish, lean, handsome, as elegant as the German shepherd dogs that had put his Etonhill Kennels on top of the heap. David had been tremendously impressed when he met the millionaire at his home in California, for, despite an aura of taste and refinement, Walter Eton was easy to know.

"Congratulations, David!"

Eton's man-to-man hand shake made David swell with importance. He stammered his thanks and proudly introduced his family and Johnny to the California man. "Gee,

Mr. Eton," he said, "I didn't suppose you ever came to Montana."

The famous breeder smiled. "I had some business in Chicago. This was not too far out of my way. After seeing Blitz three weeks ago, I rather hoped to see her show. I believe she's going to be Etonhill's next champion."

"She'll have to win the Group to get anywhere," David said soberly. "She only gets two points for her win in German shepherds. And that boxer that beat her in Billings is here in Bozeman."

"Different judges, though," observed Price Sargent. "Blitz is a better dog than that boxer. I've seen him in other shows. Actually, I'd be more afraid of the corgi that Bill Rawleigh is handling."

"When do they judge this so-called group?" Dad asked.

"It'll be late this afternoon, after all the different breeds have been judged," Johnny said. "If they take them in order, they'll start with the Sporting Dogs, then the Hounds—then—"

"Hold on! How many groups are there?"

"Six," David supplied.

"I never realized there was so much to a dog show," Dad confessed.

Price Sargent and Mr. Eton left to put Squire away, and the Hollises drifted over to watch events in the obedience ring. Since the rescue of Winston Grosser, Dad had changed his attitude about obedience training. Several times David had seen him looking out the window when the boys were working Shad and Blitz in the yard.

Neither David nor Johnny were scheduled to compete until afternoon, but Johnny was the second handler in the ring after the lunch break. For once Shad did everything right. David figured him for at least a 194, but when the winning scores were announced at the conclusion of the Open A class, the judge had marked him down to a disappointing 188. "You've been robbed!" David exclaimed.

Johnny shrugged. "The best dog in the class only got 193, and I thought he looked real good."

A stranger sitting near them swiveled to join their conversation. "This is a tough judge," he said. "He's never given a perfect score. Everybody's griping about their low scores."

"Aw, I'm not griping . . . not really," said Johnny with a grin. "I got a leg."

Before David was due in the ring with Blitz for Novice B, he took her for a short walk. He had noticed in Billings that the tension of the show and the long wait before going into the ring had seemed to blunt her enthusiasm. Unlike Johnny, he couldn't be satisfied merely to pass the test and earn a leg. He wanted to win a trophy. He hoped he would never be guilty of poor sportsmanship, but he did like to win. When the steward called his number, he was ready and Blitz was sharp.

The familiar first exercise was the Heel on Leash. David gambled. From the moment he moved forward on the judge's first command until the final halt and "exercise finished," he did not so much as glance at his dog. He sensed rather than saw her at his side. Deliberately, he gave the impression that he had absolute faith in her.

On the Stand for Examination, when he removed the leash and stepped away, Blitz stood boldly but regally aloof. She looked at David, as she should, and for her the judge did not exist.

In the Heel Free exercise, David thought twice that

Blitz lagged, once on an about turn and again on the fast
pace. However, he kept his eyes straight ahead, and on
the final halt he looked down to see the dog sitting
squarely beside him. "Good dog!" he cried.

For the Recall, he took Blitz to the far end of the ring.
This was the big one. Blitz loved to come. She could
scarcely wait for him to give the command. Although she
never had actually broken, sometimes she would anticipate. She would half-start, then settle back on her haunches.

"Leave your dog."

David used the threatening voice he used when Muggins chased the neighbor's cat and Blitz thought she
might like to join the fun. "*Stay!*"

He made the long walk and turned, hoping his apprehension did not show. Blitz ran out her tongue in an eager
grin.

"Call your dog."

"Blitz, come!"

Like a guided missile she came straight in and sat in
front. Waiting for the command to finish, she moved
smartly to the heel position. The gallery applauded as
David bent to praise her. "That's a well-trained shepherd," the judge conceded, cracking a smile for the first
time since David entered the ring.

The next contestant, a woman from Oregon whom
David had met in Bilings, congratulated him as he came
out the gate. "That's the high score in the trial so far!" she
said with enthusiasm.

David grinned. "Thanks, but I'm afraid she lagged on
me off lead."

"No, she didn't, David," Johnny butted in. "She was
right with you all the time."

David wished the woman luck with her miniature poodle and walked over to rejoin his parents. "I don't understand all that I know about obedience," Dad said, "but Blitz looked just about perfect to me."

"David," Johnny declared, "she looked as sharp as Flash did that time at Idaho Falls."

When the last dog had completed the individual portion of the Novice B test, all fifteen contestants were called back into the ring for the one-minute Long Sit and the three-minute Long Down. David had one bad moment when a Weimaraner next to Blitz broke the Sit and wandered over to root at Blitz with his nose. Blitz ignored the ill-mannered stranger, however, and a steward quickly led him away.

The whole class was asked to remain in the ring for the awarding of the prizes and ribbons. The owner of the Weimaraner sighed. "There's no point in this jug-head staying," he remarked to David. "Your dog or that black standard poodle is going to be first."

The judge completed totaling the scores, then turned to address the contestants. "Will dog number 122 and dog number 150 please come to the judge's table."

"122—that's you," said the woman with the miniature poodle on David's left. "I bet you tied."

A moment later the judge confirmed her suspicion. "Dog 150, a black standard poodle, and dog 122, a German shepherd, have earned identical scores. To determine which one shall receive the higher placing, both shall, in accordance with American Kennel Club obedience regulations, perform the same exercise at the same time. I have chosen the Recall exercise."

As David took his place beside the man with the

poodle, every nerve in his body seemed to be trembling with nervous excitement. "Are you ready?" asked the judge. "Leave your dogs!"

David put his left hand in front of Blitz' muzzle, palm back. "Stay!" he heard the poodle man say, but incredibly from his own mouth came the word, "Heel!" He knew the instant he uttered it that he had given the wrong command. His gasp of dismay was echoed by a hundred spectators.

Numb with shock, David started forward. He took half a dozen steps, then glanced back. Blitz stood half-crouched, undecided as to whether to heed the hand signal or obey the voice command. Finally, with head lowered, she slunk to catch up.

"Exercise finished," said the judge. "Tough luck, son."

A few moments later the scores for the class were announced. The black standard poodle had earned 199½ "plus" out of a possible 200. Blitz had earned 199½. David shook his head as he walked out of the ring with his second-place trophy. "Talk about stupid!"

Johnny clapped him on the shoulder. "Join the club! The rest of us have been making handling errors for years!"

He sounded so cheerful that David looked at him in surprise. Was Johnny glad he'd blown the chance to win High Score in Trial? Was Johnny jealous? Well, maybe, David thought suddenly, it wasn't fun always to be second-best. His friend never had won a trophy.

As if reading his thoughts, Johnny said, "Aw, I'm sorry, David. That was a rough one to lose."

David punched his friend on the arm. "Bet I don't do that again in the next thousand years."

The judging of the six Variety Groups began shortly thereafter. When the Working breeds were called, David and Blitz entered the ring with thirteen other dogs and handlers. Each dog had been chosen the best of his particular breed among the entries in this show. Many of these were champions, but two or three were mediocre dogs that had advanced to the Group only because they had had little or no competition on the breed level.

The Group judge was not the same man who had picked Blitz over the other German shepherds that morning. A big fellow, white-haired and slow-moving, he seemed to have trouble bending and stooping. Yet he was thorough. Just as in the breed judging, he moved the whole class, then had them gait individually. Painstakingly, he examined each dog. At last he seemed about to make his selections. He walked very slowly down the line of dogs, each one stacked to the best of his handler's ability.

David resisted the impulse to keep fiddling with his dog, to reposition a foot, to lift the muzzle a quarter of an inch. At the exact moment the judge looked his way, he said softly, "Where's Muggins!" and Blitz tensed, a statue come to life.

The judge moved on to the end of the line and then shuffled back. "I want to see the boxer and the corgi again," he said. "Take them around, please."

David released a long breath. As the tension drained out of him, he felt unutterably weary. Price Sargent had thought Blitz could win the Group. Apparently either Blitz wasn't that good, or else David wasn't the handler he was supposed to be.

The boxer and the Pembroke Welsh corgi made their

circle and returned to their places. Suddenly the judge was pointing at David. "One," he said. He pointed to the corgi. "Two." Three was the boxer, and he placed an old English sheepdog fourth.

Blitz had won!

When David came out of the ring, still half-blinded by the flashbulb of the photographer, his folks and Harvey, Price Sargent, Mr. Eton, and Johnny were all waiting to pound him on the back. He was still grinning foolishly, too excited to talk, when Murray Williams came striding around from the far side of the auditorium to add his good wishes.

An hour and a half later six dogs, the six Group winners, entered an enlarged ring for the Best in Show competition. A golden retriever represented the Sporting breeds. From the Hound Group came a basset hound. An Airedale had been chosen the best Terrier. The top Toy was an Italian greyhound, and representing the Non-Sporting Group was a miniature poodle. With Blitz, a Working Dog, these were the cream of the cream.

Judging honors this time fell to the same slight, graying man who that morning had selected Blitz for Best of Breed. Because he had placed the young dog over two champions, David had high hopes. However, although the judge did look at Blitz a long time, when finally he made his decision, the golden retriever moved to the center of the ring to stand by the sign that said Best in Show.

David congratulated the winner and walked with Blitz from the ring. He was disappointed, but not really let down. Losing to the best dog in the show was no disgrace. Mostly he was just tired.

"Great going, kid," Price Sargent said, meeting him just outside the gate.

Walter Eton extended his hand. "There's a job waiting for you at Etonhill, David, anytime you want it."

"Now, just a minute!" said Murray Williams at David's elbow. "The sheriff's office over at Winnegar has already staked a claim on this boy!"

Beside the deputy sheriff, grinning a bit sheepishly, stood Dad. "He has to finish high school," he protested. "You know. I always told him he was wasting his time fooling with dogs."

"Not this kid," averred Sargent.

Eton smiled. "When Blitz has her litter, David, I want you to pick out a pup for yourself. You've done an outstanding job training, conditioning, and handling."

David thanked the millionaire. "But I don't want a puppy," he said. "I want Blitz. I'm glad to keep her for you, of course, but some day I'd like to own her for myself."

"Well, I'll just make you a deal, David," Eton replied. "The day you sign a contract and come to work for me, I'll give you Blitz. And that is a promise."

"That is unfair competition," observed Deputy Sheriff Murray Williams.

Just then a cold nose thrust into David's hand. He looked down and suddenly, as happiness overwhelmed him, he couldn't see too well. Kneeling quickly, he buried his face in the dense coat of the exuberant shepherd.

About the Author

Born a Westerner and a Montanan by choice, Jo Sykes has held a rather unique assortment of jobs. She has been a cowhand, a combination packer-guide-cook in a hunting camp, a surveyor's assistant, and an instructor of dog obedience classes. She began writing seriously at the age of thirteen and has six published books to her credit, including *Trouble Creek* and *Wolf Dog of Ambush Canyon*. Miss Sykes presently lives in Livingston, Montana.